DREAM OF ME

By Lindsay McKenna

Blue Turtle Publishing

Praise for Lindsay McKenna

"A treasure of a book... highly recommended reading that everyone will enjoy and learn from."

—Chief Michael Jaco, US Navy SEAL, retired, on Breaking Point

"Readers will root for this complex heroine, scarred both inside and out, and hope she finds peace with her steadfast and loving hero. Rife with realistic conflict and spiced with danger, this is a worthy page-turner."

—BookPage.com on Taking Fire
March 2015 Top Pick in Romance

"... is fast-paced romantic suspense that renders a beautiful love story, start to finish. McKenna's writing is flawless, and her story line fully absorbing. More, please."

—Annalisa Pesek, Library Journal on Taking Fire

"Ms. McKenna masterfully blends the two different paces to convey a beautiful saga about love, trust, patience and having faith in each other."

—Fresh Fiction on Never Surrender

"Genuine and moving, this romantic story set in the complex world of military ops grabs at the heart."

—RT Book Reviews on Risk Taker

"McKenna does a beautiful job of illustrating difficult topics through the development of well-formed, sympathetic characters."

—Publisher's Weekly (starred review) on Wolf Haven
One of the Best Books of 2014, Publisher's Weekly

"McKenna delivers a story that is raw and heartfelt. The relationship between Kell and Leah is both passionate and tender. Kell is the hero every woman wants, and McKenna employs skill and empathy to craft a physically and emotionally abused character in Leah. Using tension and steady pacing, McKenna is adept at expressing growing, tender love in the midst of high stakes danger."

—RT Book Reviews on Taking Fire

"Her military background lends authenticity to this outstanding tale, and readers will fall in love with the upstanding hero and his fierce determination to save the woman he loves.

—Publishers Weekly (starred review) on Never Surrender
One of the Best Books of 2014, Publisher's Weekly

"Readers will find this addition to the Shadow Warriors series full of intensity and action-packed romance. There is great chemistry between the characters and tremendous realism, making Breaking Point a great read."

—RT Book Reviews

"This sequel to Risk Taker is an action-packed, compelling story, and the sizzling chemistry between Ethan and Sarah makes this a good read."

—RT Book Reviews on Degree of Risk

"McKenna elicits tears, laughter, fist-pumping triumph, and most all, a desire for the next tale in this powerful series."

—Publishers Weekly (starred review) on Running Fire

"McKenna's military experience shines through in this moving tale ... McKenna (High Country Rebel) skillfully takes readers on an emotional journey into modern warfare and two people's hearts."

—Publisher's Weekly on Down Range

"Lindsay McKenna has proven that she knows what she's doing when it comes to these military action/romance books."

—Terry Lynn, Amazon on Zone of Fire.

"At no time do you want to put your book down and come back to it later! Last Chance is a well written, fast paced, short (remember that) story that will please any military romance reader!"

—LBDDiaries, Amazon on Last Chance.

Available from
Lindsay McKenna

Blue Turtle Publishing

DELOS

Last Chance, prologue novella to Nowhere to Hide
Nowhere to Hide, Book 1
Tangled Pursuit, Book 2
Forged in Fire, Book 3

2016

Broken Dreams, Book 4
Cowboy Justice Bundle/Blind Sided, Bundle 2, novella
Blind Sided, BN2
Secret Dream, B1B novella, epilogue to Nowhere to Hide
Hold On, Book 5
Hold Me, 5B1, sequel to Hold On
Unbound Pursuit, 2B1 novella, epilogue to Tangled Pursuit
Dog Tags for Christmas Bundle/Snowflake's Gift, Bundle 3,
novella
Secrets, 2B2 novella, sequel to Unbound Pursuit, 2B1

2017

Snowflake's Gift, Book 6
Never Enough, 3B1, novella, sequel to Forged in Fire
Dream of Me, 4B1, novella, sequel to Broken Dreams
Trapped, Book 7
Taking a Chance, Book 8, sequel to Trapped

Harlequin/HQN/Harlequin Romantic Suspense

SHADOW WARRIORS
Danger Close
Down Range
Risk Taker
Degree of Risk
Breaking Point
Never Surrender
Zone of Fire
Taking Fire
On Fire
Running Fire

THE WYOMING SERIES
Shadows From The Past
Deadly Identity
Deadly Silence
The Last Cowboy
The Wrangler
The Defender
The Loner
High Country Rebel
Wolf Haven
Night Hawk
Out Rider

WIND RIVER VALLEY SERIES, Kensington

2016
Wind River Wrangler
Wind River Rancher

2017
Wind River Cowboy
Wind River Wrangler's Challenge

Dream of Me

This is a work of fiction. Names, characters, places and incidents are either the product of the author's imagination or are used fictitiously, and any resemblance to actual persons, living or dead, business establishments, events or locales is entirely coincidental.

This edition published by arrangement with Blue Turtle Publishing

www.lindsaymckenna.com

Dear Reader,

Welcome to the Delos Series! You met Alexa Culver and Gage Hunter in *Broken Dreams*. Now readers get to follow Alexa and Gage's continuing story in *Dream of Me*.

Alexa has left the US Air Force as an A-10 combat pilot, and moved to Artemis, the in-house security firm for all the Delos charities. She is the director of the safe house arm of Delos, which works to protect women and their children who have been abused, placed into sex slavery or family abuse. She's a crusader for women, wanting to protect them; to give them a safe place for themselves and their frightened children. Being of service, making a difference in the world drives Alexa, who is often compared to her mother Dilara Culver, who is the CEO of Delos.

Alexa understands first-hand the trauma, due to her own capture by a Pakistani raid in an Afghan village (*Broken Dreams*, Book 4). Due to her experience, she now suffers from PTSD. Gage, who lives with her at their farmhouse outside of Alexandria, Virginia, is worried for Alexa. He sees that the PTSD symptoms from her capture and sexual abuse, runs her life now. Their own relationship is an up-and-down emotional roller coaster as a result. Gage loves Alexa. He would do anything in the world to give her a sense of safety and being protected. But her

Type A personality, her driving need to help others, places her squarely in the face of danger once again. Can he save her? Save their relationship?

Let me hear from you about the Culver Family and the Delos series. Please visit my website at www.lindsaymckenna.com, to keep up the latest, exciting happenings with my series.

You will find an excerpt in the back of this novella for *Trapped*, Ali and Ram's story.

Happy reading!
Warmly, Lindsay McKenna

Dedication

To my wonderful reviewers who are also readers of Delos—thank you for ALL your hard work in penning a review on the latest book of mine you have read! Some (but not all) are named here: L. M. Landau, Jan Kaplan, GDS, Sandra Van Winkle, Ladee Aqua, Therese Lopez, Sunny FLA, Stacey, and Viki Ferrell, plus so many others for whom I am grateful! Thank you!

CHAPTER 1

"**G**OING ON A hike was *such* a great idea of yours, Gage," Alexa Culver said, her spirits high as she looked back at him as they hiked a trail deep in the Virginia woodlands. Around her, late September leaves were turning red, yellow, and orange. Some drifted down toward them, creating a picture-perfect fall morning. They had just reached the top of a large hill above their recently purchased 1850s farmhouse.

"Anywhere with you is always a great idea." Gage grinned as he picked his way along the steep, rocky trail covered with crunchy, dry leaves. The eighty-degree morning breeze swirled playfully around them as he caught up with Alexa, watching as she absently tucked her auburn hair behind her ears.

Today, Gage was wearing fitted jeans that

emphasized his lean, tall body. Alexa always
appreciated his lithe energy: like a cougar, he
prowled rather than walked. She recognized this
was partly from his training as a Marine Corps
sniper, but it was also an inborn quality that had
served them both well recently.

Even when they'd met last November at the
Bagram Army base north of Kabul, Afghanistan's
capital, she'd been aware of the powerful,
undiluted sexual chemistry between them. But
she had never imagined that in a few short days,
Gage and his SEAL team would rescue her and
eight other women from the Taliban. Since that
time, they had grown even closer to each other,
and were now back home in the States working
for Artemis Security. It was the hidden security
branch within Delos, the largest global charity.

But those terrifying, life-changing events had
been indelibly burned into Alexa's memory. She
tried to bury them by working longer, harder
hours—in fact, she was in the office seven days a
week, and found that when she was focusing on
being director of Artemis's Safe House Foundation, she could crowd them out. Whether she
could ever completely heal from those two
devastating days, during which she had endured
verbal abuse, assault, beatings, and nonstop
sexual humiliation, no one could guess.

Now, Gage slowed his pace, his long fingers
wrapped around the red shoulder straps of the

large knapsack he carried on his back. "You look as if you belong out here," he said, leaning over to brush her smiling lips with a kiss. His body, as always, hungered for Alexa. He'd missed making love to her, but because she'd been so devastated by her capture by the Taliban, he'd told her he would wait until she was ready to be intimate again.

Gage never kidded himself that he could read a woman's mind, but he did know Alexa well enough to read her body language. Today, she looked particularly attractive in her white shorts and a sleeveless cotton tee the color of her auburn hair. She was free of makeup, and he saw the light sprinkling of girlish freckles peeking out across her cheeks.

He loved her. Gage knew her so well that he could read her moods from her eyes. He had learned that when the brown flecks in her eyes were prominent, she was emotionally upset about something. But if the green and gold were front and center, she was happy and at peace.

"Look at this," he said, leaning down and capturing a red leaf at their feet. Holding it up, he brought it near her ponytail lying on her right shoulder. "The colors almost match," he said, placing the recently dropped leaf next to her hair. Gage drew in her scent, which made his growing erection harden even more. Alexa gazed down at it, a playful look on her face; both were aware that they'd had no sex together for five days.

Now, she stepped forward and pressed her breasts against his chest. Unable to resist, Gage pulled her to him and captured her mouth, now soft and willing beneath his. Reluctantly easing away from her, drowning in those green-flecked eyes that showed how much she loved him, Gage breathed in the scent of almond oil in her hair, a fragrance that always aroused him.

Alexa's mother, Dilara, who was Turkish with a bit of Greek, put a few drops in her own hair every morning to make it shine, and her daughter tended to follow her mother's example—from her high-fashion clothing, to her perfect makeup and skillfully arranged coiffure.

"Wow," Alexa laughed. "That's quite a match." Her eyes crinkled with humor as she examined the leaf. "Hey, are you calling me a dried up old leaf, Hunter?"

He chuckled. "Not hardly, Ms. Culver." His heart swelled. It was rare, since her capture and rescue, that the Alexa he'd met and fallen in love with had resurfaced. And the wicked smile on those beautifully shaped lips, combined with the dancing glint in her eyes, boded well.

Gage silently congratulated himself on having dragged Alexa kicking and screaming away from the office for this noontime hike up into the hills. She had been getting ready at nine a.m. on Saturday to drive into work, but her face reflected the strain she was under. Gage had avoided telling Alexa what to do since her ordeal with the Taliban, whenever possible urging her to take control of her activities. But this time, he was damn glad he'd coaxed her into taking this five-mile hike into the Virginia hills above their farmhouse. Already, the strain and smudges around her eyes were gone. The young woman standing before him right now was the Alexa he'd met at Bagram, and he couldn't feel more grateful to have her back.

"It's beautiful up here," Alexa breathed, gesturing around the hilltop crowned with colorful trees. The sky was a deep marine blue with a few fluffy clouds drifting overhead. Breathing in deeply, she leaned against him, her hand on his chest, looking skyward. "I love the smell of autumn leaves, Gage." Turning, she gazed at his ruggedly handsome face, his light blue eyes warm with love.

"Do you wish you were flying your Stearman biplane instead of being chained here to the earth?" he teased, lifting his hand to graze her rosy cheek with his thumb. His touch always aroused her, and he watched her pupils grow larger, her lips part. He fought his desire to take her right there. They had been together for five days, and it hadn't been the right time or place to resume their steamy connection.

"I don't know," Alexa murmured. "It's a perfect day to fly. But right now," she smiled as she moved her hips suggestively against the thick bulge beneath his jeans, "I like being earthbound with you." Alexa saw how Gage's expression changed from loving to lusty, and it made her inner thighs dampen even more. She grazed his recently shaven cheek, feeling completely loved and cared for as he tightened his arm around her shoulder. Slowly moving so their hips touched, she pinned herself against him. "I can't really pilot the Stearman and make love with you at the same time."

"Hmm," Gage said, giving her a crooked grin. His long fingers caressed her sweet, rounded cheeks beneath her flimsy white cotton shorts. "If you had a choice, Ms. Culver, which would you prefer: making love with me, or flying into the arms of your beloved sky?" He saw her eyes crinkle, that wicked look deepening in her hazel eyes.

"Oh, my choice would always be you, Mr. Hunter. I've never met a man who could love me as wonderfully as you do."

In response, he leaned over and nibbled on her ear lobe, feeling her breath draw swiftly inward, knowing it was giving her pleasure. She moaned as he continued to nip, kiss, and then lick his way down her exposed slender neck, her hips grinding against his. Yes, his woman was hungry for some great sex, and so was he. But with Alexa, Gage never called it "sex," because it was a hundred times more powerful than two people simply getting physical pleasure.

Since her capture, Alexa was aware that the desire to make love with Gage came and went, mostly depending upon moods that she could not control. When she was in a "down cycle," she sometimes couldn't even let Gage touch her. That was when he knew she was reliving the horror she'd experienced within the Taliban caves in Afghanistan. Then, usually about three days later, she'd cycle up again and return to the Alexa she'd been before her capture.

"Then," Gage rasped, moving his tongue over the arch of her delicate ear, "you have another big decision to make. It's almost noon. Are you hungry for food, or for something else?" He heard her breathy sigh as her hand wrapped across his bulge beneath his jeans. Groaning, he caressed her butt, moving his finger down the crease, hearing her gasp with anticipation.

From the beginning, Alexa had brought out the hugger, toucher, and embracer in him. She had helped him heal from his own dark past so much so that it astounded him at times. Her natural warmth, her caring, and her need for a loving physical connection opened his heart in ways it never had before. Yes, Alexa was a sensual, highly erotic woman, and she genuinely enjoyed the pleasure her body received from him, but since her capture lovemaking had been erratic.

Right now, however, she was that sleek, sensual, purring animal who aroused him immediately, and she was ready for him. He could see it in her eyes and the movements of her body.

The day was perfect, Gage decided, loosening his embrace with her, allowing his hand to move between her thighs, close to her crotch, feeling the dampness there. His cock jerked in response, trapped in the tight, tough fabric of his jeans.

Alexa continued to caress his erection, driving him nearly insane with the need to plunge inside her. She looked around and said, "Hey, I see a really nice place to put down our blanket. Over there." She lifted her hand away from his crotch to point at the very top of the hill.

"Hmm, looks like a well-protected spot, speaking as a sniper," he suggested, easing her beneath his arm and walking her in that direction. Alexa slipped her arm around his waist, languidly leaning against him.

"Who better to trust for a hiding spot than a sniper, right?" She laughed, nuzzling into his chest, kissing his damp red T-shirt. Gage was the sexiest-looking man she'd ever seen in jeans and a tee. It oozed out of his pores naturally. He always claimed he didn't realize it, but as a woman, she could sense it a mile away.

When she'd been an A-10 combat pilot, a captain in the Air Force, and had met Gage, a Marine Corps sniper, she hadn't cared that the man was enlisted and she was an officer. He'd drawn her to him like a powerful, sexual magnet.

Then she discovered that he was kind, tender, and sensitive. He never treated her like an object, someone whose value was merely sexual. Nor did he think he was superior because he was a man. Gage had always treated her like an equal, his attitude a gift he was given by his very loving parents. His Marine Corps sniper father had openly shown affection, love, respect, and equality to his wife and their children, and Alexa silently blessed his now deceased parents. They had given Gage a healthy model for how to treat women, and for that, Alexa would be eternally grateful.

Gage slid a look down at her. "It's a good position," he agreed. The place he had brought her to was a circle of brush eight to ten feet tall on the crown of the hill, where the vegetation received a lot of sunlight. There was an entry point to the brush, and he led her into it, looking around. It reminded him of the caves of Afghanistan, and he suddenly felt concerned, watching Alexa's face as she gazed around the enclosure. He was unsure how she'd take the fairly intimate, walled area.

"Perfect," Alexa declared, releasing him. "Come on, I'll open that ruck you're wearing and pull out the blanket."

Relief swept through him, and he turned toward her as she unzipped the back. "Like it, huh?"

"Yes, it hides us well."

He arched an eyebrow. "And who is going to stop you from screaming when you have your first of many orgasms?"

She giggled and pulled out the bright green wool blanket from the ruck. "No one! You said this was the highest hill around and that there were no houses nearby."

Chuckling, he eased out of the ruck and set it near the thicket wall. Alexa joined him in picking up two ends of the blanket and spreading it out in the center of the grass, away from rocks or fallen tree limbs. "I did say that, but you know—shrieks of pleasure do have a way of being carried in the wind."

"Well," she pouted, smoothing out the blanket. "Who's going to hear it? The trees? The cows down below over in that farmer's field?"

"Okay by me," Gage murmured, giving her a burning look that made her lick her lower lip. His cock was killing him. "So what are we waiting for? Let's get undressed." He pulled the red T-shirt over his head, his toned chest and firm belly made Alexa hungrier than ever for him.

"You have the most beautiful chest and shoulders, Gage Hunter," she admired, moving toward him and splaying her fingers across his lightly dusted chest. Leaning forward, she licked one of his nipples and he froze, then groaned as she continued to lick and then lightly nibble it.

"Baby," he pleaded, easing her away. "I won't last another minute with a frontal assault like that."

Making a pitying sound in the back of her throat, Alexa stepped away and met his feral gaze. "Well, hurry up!" she laughed. "Last person undressed is a rotten egg!"

With that, she pulled her tee over her head, revealing that she hadn't worn a bra. Had she been planning this?

Gage fumbled with the metal snap on his jeans. "No fair!"

"Gotcha!" Alexa laughed, shimmying swiftly out of her shorts. She'd worn no panties, either. In seconds, she'd pushed off her tennis shoes, standing proudly naked before him, her hands on her waist, grinning.

Giving her a dark look, Gage grumbled as he opened and unzipped his jeans. "Okay, you beat me. I concede to the world's fastest stripper."

"Ohh," Alexa said, looking at his erection pop out of the opened zipper. "I think I'm the winner here." She stepped forward and slid her hands around him before he had pushed his jeans down over his hard, curved thighs. Gliding her fingers up and down the warm, hard velvet shaft, she gave him a coy look. "You have the most beautiful cock, Gage. I know I've told you that before, but . . ." she sighed, lightly moving her fingertip over the crest, "you are a beautifully built man."

Gritting his teeth, he stayed frozen in place as Alexa's soft, exploring fingers, delicate and sensitive, wrapped around his aching erection. She'd damn near made him come, and Gage was already leaking like a sieve. That was the kind of effect she had on him.

"I'm not going to get undressed unless you let me go," he told her gruffly, leaning over and giving her a swift, hot kiss on her smiling lips.

"Okay," she murmured, reluctantly releasing him. "I'll be a good girl."

He snorted in disbelief and finished stripping. Then he grabbed her, hauling her slender body against his. She laughed, rubbing her pelvis against his straining cock, sending boiling heat licking through him.

"You are *such* a tease," he rasped, nipping her neck just enough to make her want to dodge him. Gage would never cause her pain, but he knew how to create intense, building pleasure in her highly sensitive erogenous zones.

"Me? A tease?" Alexa said, her smile widening as she slid her arms around his shoulders, feeling him hardening, knowing he wanted her as badly as she wanted him. Rubbing her belly against his trapped erection, she focused on the intensity of his eyes, the combination lover/sniper/hunter that would always be within him. "I just know what I like, Hunter. What about you?"

Gage had to laugh out loud as she gave him that innocent look of hers. Alexa, a tough, aggressive combat pilot, wasn't at all shy about going after what she wanted and taking it. She was a type A personality; but then, so was he.

"Well," he said, lifting her off her feet and into his arms, "let's get down to business, shall we?"

Her breathy laughter promised him dizzying pleasures ahead, and he wanted to be inside her now, surrounded by her thick, warm juices, and stay there forever. They had many things in common, among them strong sex drives that brought them both to climax again and again.

Gently depositing her on the blanket, he watched as Alexa lifted herself up just enough to pull him down on the blanket beside her, urging him onto his back. Gage saw the combat pilot in her expression now, as if she were getting ready to make a bombing run. His whole body flexed in anticipation. After five days of abstinence, both of them felt like boiling teakettles about to spill over.

"I'm today's target of opportunity, huh?" he asked as she straddled his hips with her long, firm thighs.

"Yes, indeed," she breathed, rubbing her wet core against his upright cock, making a low, satisfied sound in her throat. She splayed out her palms on his chest, slowly rubbing up and down on him, watching his eyes half close, and smiling as he couldn't hold back any longer, releasing a hoarse moan. "Oh, baby," he groaned, reaching for her.

"Uh-huh," she said. "Keep your hands at your sides, Hunter. You can't touch me. I want you to lie still."

Grimacing, he muttered, "That will be pure hell for me."

She closed her eyes. "Just for a little while. I feel so much pressure inside me, Gage, and I need to come . . . soon . . ."

Gage nodded, "I need to touch you, Alexa." He slid his hands over her hips, helping her move, bringing down more pressure upon her body, rubbing her firmly onto his cock. He fought not to come, closing his eyes and gritting his teeth. "Ride me, baby . . . ride me . . ."

Gage damn near lost control as she settled against his wet, slick shaft. He was dying to taste her, kiss her, and suck her nipples. His body was on fire as she worked him over.

Alexa closed her eyes, her chin tipped upward, a sweet smile on her parted lips revealing how much pleasure she was taking for herself as she rocked back and forth on him. Every woman with experience knew that riding a man's cock was the surest way to a swift, intense orgasm.

At this point, Alexa didn't even have to be entered to accomplish the next stage: his thick, warm erection moved against her swollen, aching clit, in perfect alignment for an explosion. And it came suddenly, making her cry out.

Gage felt her thighs tighten around his hips as a low, keening sound began deep within her. A rush of moist, hot juices spilled over him and Alexa froze, unable to move as the powerful orgasm swept through her in undulating rhythm as he slid her back and forth. Gage knew how to milk her body, even if she couldn't move, making her pleasure almost unbearably intense. More than anything, he wanted his brave, beautiful woman to be thrown into that faraway land of magic, heat, and soaring pleasure.

Spent, Alexa finally crumpled, lying down beside him so her brow nestled next to his neck and jaw, breathing raggedly. Her hand weakly opened and closed against his other shoulder.

Gage had a typical sniper's patience and allowed Alexa time to stop trembling, meanwhile releasing small cries of pleasure. Her breathing was chaotic, punctuated by more happy, little sounds caught in her throat. As he gentled her heaving, quivering body, hand open and palm flat, lightly skimming her long spine, he kissed her hair. The scent of her sex almost undid him, but he controlled himself for her sake. There were few things that made her terrible memories go away and gave her some peace. Having an orgasm was one of them. The other was Gage's slow, sensual loving.

Finally, the warmth of the noontime breeze, mixed with the scent of drying leaves on the dirt floor around them, conspired to soothe her as well. Gage kept his touch feather light as he grazed her damp shoulders and back. Alexa clung to him as if afraid that if she let go of him, she would lose him forever.

Gage knew it was a result of her kidnapping, being tied down to a steel gurney and sexually assaulted. Sometimes when he slept, he would awaken and find her clinging to him like a life raft. It was then that he knew she was caught up in another nightmare, little whimpers of terror coming from deep within. He would soothe her with his hands, his body curving protectively around hers, claiming her with his low, calming voice. Then, Alexa would begin to relax, stop clinging to him, and surrender to sleep instead.

Gage did the same now, wanting to lull her, maybe allow her to fall asleep with him and make up for all the sleep she lost nightly. He doubted she slept more than three or four hours a night, and it was broken, light sleep at that. Alexa was battling the monsters who had murdered part of her soul. She would never get that destroyed piece back, but Gage could be there to help her heal the rest of the emotional fractures that reminded her of the experience.

And little by little, Alexa was healing. But as a combat pilot who made things happen in a split second within the cockpit of her A-10, she was learning that life on the ground was very different.

Gage sensed her frustration with herself, always down upon herself, always expecting more, and far too quickly.

An assaulted body, brain, heart, and emotions took time to heal. Gage knew that because his sister, Jen, and his father had been torn from him and his mother. It took seven years for him to come to terms with the worst of the shock that day. Then, while Gage was in the Marine Corps, his mother had suddenly died and he was left with no family, only photos and memories.

Gage kissed Alexa's mussed hair, feeling her burrow her face against his jaw. A soft smile tugged at his mouth as he continued to caress her hair, and with his other hand hold her protectively. She responded well to both, and he was grateful. "Okay?" he whispered in her ear, feeling her breathing shallow out.

"Mmm . . . that felt so good, Gage . . . thank

you . . . thank you so much . . ."

Closing his eyes, he breathed deep and brought her sexy fragrance into his lungs. "Feel a little relief now?" He could hear the sleepiness in her voice and knew just how tired she really was.

"Mmm . . . much . . . better . . ." and her words slipped away.

Smiling to himself, Gage felt her entire body relax. She felt like a sweet, warm blanket placed over him. Alexa trusted him, and for that he was ever so grateful. He'd been afraid after her trauma that she would always see in him the Pakistani men who had assaulted her. Fortunately, she didn't.

Tal, her older sister, agreed with Becka, the Artemis psychiatrist—because Alexa had fully trusted Gage before the assault, her brain still saw him as a "safe" male. Someone who would not hurt her. Alexa was such a little thing against him, sweet, relaxed, her moist breath soft and feathery against his neck. Often, Alexa would sleep after making love with him. It was a time when those arousing hormones cascaded down through her lower body, chased the anxiety away, neutralized it, and left her in a small corner of peace. Gage wished with all his heart he could absorb the painful memories of Alexa's assault so she could be free of all her PTSD symptoms. But he couldn't.

The birds were singing around them, the

breeze light as it slipped through the tall wall of thickets. The smell of decaying leaves was one of Gage's favorite autumn fragrances. He rested his hand against the center of her back, her flesh now air-dried. Today had turned out special, and Gage was so glad he'd been able to coax Alexa out into nature, rather than working all day at Artemis.

A blue jay called raucously from a nearby hill. The wind blew a little more, sending down a shower of new leaves twirling and dancing in the arms of the breeze. Gage was content. All he wanted out of his life since meeting Alexa was to love her, marry her, and settle in and eventually become parents. A faint smile tugged at his mouth. Alexa was such a mothering type. It was part of what drew him to her—her large, giving heart and genuine love of people, always trying to alleviate their suffering.

They'd just bought their farmhouse and were enjoying the process of looking for just the right antique furniture to fill it with. His mother's engagement ring sat on the ring finger of Alexa's left hand. Their commitment to one another was solid. Only this damned hormone assault was the monster that kept invading her daily world, anxiety ripping through her. When would her memory allow her some peace? When would those nightmares leave her alone?

Becka had told both of them that dreams and

nightmares were a safe way for the experience to work its way out of one's psyche. As time passed, it would be less intense and come up less often until finally, someday, months or years later, it would finally work out of her emotions and she would eventually find some level of peace.

How Gage wanted that day to come sooner than later. He lived to hear Alexa laugh, to see life in her large, intelligent hazel eyes shine once more. He wanted peace for her. Today was a gift, and he relished it. Today, he had the old Alexa back. The day wasn't over, but he wasn't going to rush Alexa or wake her up so she could eat lunch.

As a sniper, he had a unique sense of time. He could stretch it, bend it, or shorten it as he needed. What Alexa needed right now was deep, uninterrupted sleep and he was more than happy to be the mattress she lay upon. He held her in his arms because it made her feel safe. He didn't care if he lay like this for the next five hours if it meant Alexa would sleep the sleep of angels— because she was one.

CHAPTER 2

G AGE FELT ALEXA stir after sleeping beside him for nearly an hour. She nuzzled him in her sleep, her hand curving around his neck, as if trying to get closer to him. His eyes turned soft with love as he looked down at her, reminded of a secure, untroubled child awakening slowly from a delicious, deep slumber. He remembered when he was young, emerging from sleep the same way. Just seeing Alexa awaken slowly, not jerking awake with a cry of alarm, was rare. Over the last month that they'd started living together, Gage could count on one hand when that had happened.

Because he was so in love with her, he was sensitive to her every mood and response. They shared a rare connection, and he was eager to discover more about how their journey together was going to develop.

Alexa could walk into his office at Artemis, and he'd know without even looking up from his desk whether she was worried, super-busy, or feeling positive about life. Sliding his hand down across her shoulder, feeling those firm muscles beneath her velvety skin, made him aroused once again.

He'd forced himself to quit reacting to her sexually while she slept, but now, as she moved her hips with him still lodged deep within her, all bets were off. He felt the tightness and the slippery wetness within her as he started to grow thicker and longer once more.

Gage tried to still his sexual hunger for her, but Alexa's innocent moves while awakening had him fully aroused. He closed his eyes, connected with her on every level, feeling her soft breath against his neck, the tickle of strands of hair against his jaw as the breeze ebbed and flowed through the thicket that hid them so well. It almost felt to him as if Alexa was dropping off to sleep once more. If that was so, he would lie there forever with her.

Gage had slept some himself, but he wasn't surprised—he'd been as sleep deprived as Alexa.

"Gage . . ."

"I'm here, baby," he whispered, moving his head to the side and kissing her hair." You can sleep more if you want . . ." Gage heard her making a nondescript happy sound in her throat, and she caressed his jaw, placing a kiss against his neck.

"I love you so much, Gage . . . so much . . ."

The tremble in her husky voice filled him with the deepest joy as he heard those longed-for words.

"I love you, too. You know that, don't you?" Sometimes, Gage wondered if Alexa *did* love him. It was nothing specific, but when she was in a down cycle, she seemed disconnected from everyone, including him.

He understood this was all part of her PTSD. And when she would come up out of that dark hole, she'd often tell him "I love you" to reassure him. It was tough seeing Alexa exist in a part-time hell, much like a bipolar person would, swinging from one extreme emotion to another.

"Mmm," she said, sinuously moving her hips, sending a new wave of desire through him. "You show me every day in large and small ways, Gage Hunter . . . please, don't ever stop . . ."

Now, the little vixen was slowly moving her hips from side to side, then slowly pulling forward and then easing back down upon him. Groaning, he watched her drowsy, half-open eyes burn with arousal. Oh yeah, he was sure as hell ready to take her hard and fast, but his sniper patience won out and he gave her a feral grin.

"You're such a tease, Ms. Culver. I'm going to come if you don't stop that . . ." He slid his hands down her arms as she warmed him with a serene smile. Her hair had loosened from that ponytail and longer strands had escaped, framing her flushed cheeks, emphasizing the gold and green in her eyes. She knew exactly what she was doing to him, and if Gage hadn't been near exploding, trying to rein in his own sexual appetite for her benefit, he'd have her riding him hard and fast.

"You feel so good to me," she whispered, trailing her short fingernails down across his chest, stopping to lean down and suckle his nipples. The sweet skitter of fire spiked within her, and she relished his length and size.

"Even a sniper has limits to his patience," he warned her gruffly, gripping her hips, sliding her slowly up and down his wet, slick cock. "Are you ready for me to end my suffering, baby?"

She smiled and left his nipple, licking his lower lip, absorbing the strength, taste, and controlled power she felt around him. "I love having you inside me. Did you know that?" She searched his burning blue eyes, riveted like a falcon on its quarry. "I love that feeling in you, the hunter, the man who is going to stalk me, slowly ease up out of nowhere and then take me."

"That's going to happen in a few seconds," he growled. "Unless you do something first."

Alexa placed her lips against his, feeling his

mouth taking hers hungrily, deeply. She ground her wet core against him, feeling the throb of his cock stroking her, building that fire that was already blazing and needy. "Tell me how you want me," she demanded. Alexa loved Gage fiercely. Since her trauma, he'd let her know that she was in full control when they made love. How many men could really do what Gage had done? She moved sinuously against him, riding his cock, absorbing that thick, warm steel that was making her clit ache, making her want to burst into orgasm. She sighed, allowing herself the pure physical pleasure of sharing her body with him. Never had she had a more skilled lover than Gage. He always thought of her first and made sure she had as many orgasms as she wanted before he gifted her with his own climax.

Kissing each corner of his mouth, drowning in the ocean blue of his eyes, feeling his love surrounding her, she whispered against him, "Tell me, Gage. It's your turn. How do you want me?"

"I want—" he growled, framing her face, loosening the rest of her ponytail, watching that straight auburn hair fall around her shoulders "—to please you."

Alexa rested her lips against his, content as never before, feeling the boiling heat in her lower body as he slowly stroked her back and forth, the ultimate tease. "Come with me this time and don't hold back," she urged, sweat gleaming on her taut body.

Nipping her full lower lip, Gage rasped, "You first, then I'll come." He saw her half-closed eyes gleam with lust and love. Her perfectly formed lips tasted sweet beneath his mouth, and they both smiled at the same time.

Their trust with one another was so incredible that sometimes Gage couldn't believe it. As he drew her upward, placing her hands on his chest, watching the expression of satisfaction in her face, he could feel how very close she was to coming again. On a good day like this, Alexa had a full sexual appetite. He eased her back and forth on his cock, absorbing the lightness coming to her nearly closed eyes, her lips parting. The soft sound she was making made his heart soar, because he was gratifying her. It made the day even more special than it already was.

Her fingers tightened against his solid torso and he rocked her harder, deeper, faster. Her breath broke and she quivered, the orgasm building rapidly within her. Gage felt her tightening around him, gripping him, and he sucked air through his clenched teeth, bringing her firmly against him. Just as he thought he couldn't control himself any longer, her orgasm erupted. It felt like a white-hot volcano flaring to life as her walls contracted violently around him, making him growl.

Alexa cried out. She froze, her fingers digging spasmodically into his ribcage, sobbing his name.

And with that, his control snapped as she continued to cry out, trapped in the fiery pleasure her body was rewarding her with, no longer coherent, but lost and floating somewhere in raw, physical satiation. Gage gripped her hips hard; then he, too, was lost in the brutal heat careening down his spine, slamming into his balls tight against his body, the burning heat making him groan. He was sent spinning into fire and blinding light as his whole being was tossed into a galaxy of stars, tumbling and floating.

Alexa's cries continued and he called her name, feeling her flatten her palms against his chest, slowly falling forward across him once more, weakness beginning to invade her spent, ravished, sweet body.

How good she felt! Gage lay there, unable to get his breath, his hands lessening their hold around her soft, rounded hips. His whole body throbbed with awareness of Alexa, of being buried deeply within her incredible, giving body. He loved her more than life because she gave all of herself to him. She never shrank back or only gave a portion of herself. She was all heart, all passion, sensitive, caring. And his.

"I DON'T WANT to leave our little hideaway,"

Alexa murmured as she tugged on her socks after pulling on her jeans. She sat opposite Gage, who was slowly dressing, too.

"It's always here," he said, catching her slumberous gaze. Her cheeks were a delicate pink, her red hair deliciously mussed around her oval face, the serenity in her expression that Gage wished would always be there. But he knew it wouldn't be for long, so he was grateful for this time when her anxiety was gone.

Sometimes it lasted half a night before her anxieties attacked her again, like an animal devouring her from within. It reminded him of a parasite inside Alexa, spreading its toxic darkness, stealing her light and her natural ebullience. Gage tried to give her light every way he could, but it never seemed to be enough to put aside the terrors that eventually overtook her, running her emotions until she was upset, disoriented, and exhausted.

Alexa's lips curved faintly as she pulled on her sneakers, tying each of them with her long, slender fingers. "I love where we live, Gage. I really do."

He had pulled on his T-shirt earlier and finished tying the laces on his boots. Then, Gage urged Alexa across his legs, settling her sweet butt into his lap so she could face him. His arms and body became a cradle for her to feel safe within. He felt her utterly relax against him, her head resting on his shoulder, lids half-closed, her expression soft and stress-free. Gage tucked her in, making sure she was comfy, taking her weight, giving her that sense of safety he knew she craved. He rested his chin against her hair, his voice low.

"When I was a kid growing up at Camp Pendleton, where we lived in military housing . . ."

"Yes?"

"We got to tramp through the hills of Pendleton. Now, it was mostly rocks, yellow soil, cactus, scrub brush, but it was my backyard. When my sister, Jen, was old enough, she'd tag along." He smiled, closing his eyes, remembering his sister—a near mirror image of Alexa personality-wise. "She loved the outdoors, too. We'd sometimes hike the hills where the Force Recon Marines were working to perfect their hunting skills. I remember this one time; we came across a huge concrete watering tank. As we went over the hill, we spotted a group of six deer with their fawns beside them, drinking from it."

"Ohh!" Alexa gasped, seeing his vision as clearly as he had. "Did you get a cell phone photo of them?"

"No," he mumbled. "I was only nine, and Jen was seven. My mom always gave me a cell phone to carry in case we needed help or got lost. It was an old phone, and the battery wore down on it fast if I turned it on. So," he said, smiling a little, "Jen and I took pictures with our eyes and stored them in our hearts instead."

"Jen sounds very special," Alexa said, hearing the loss in Gage's tone. There were days when he became quiet and withdrawn, remembering his lost family. And he was especially vulnerable after loving her. These were the moments she cherished with Gage the most. She loved when he opened up and shared the happy moments he had had with his family. There was his younger sister, his heroic Marine Corps sniper father, and his mother, who was slowly going blind with macular degeneration disease. "Did you ever mind her coming along with you?"

"No," he whispered, lost in his hall of memories, his eyes closed as he held her. "Never. Jen was like you: fearless. She could hike those rugged hills of Pendleton with the best of the Marines. She never asked me to slow down. Never quit, either. Although," he drawled, laughing a little, "she'd throw a pebble at my back, letting me know that my very long legs were eating up too much ground between us!"

"She sounds a lot like you," Alexa whispered, leaning back, meeting his sad blue eyes. "I'm so glad you're sharing these times with me, Gage. You help me to know Jen better. It allows me a window into your life, into the happy times you had together."

He took his index finger, removing several auburn strands from her furrowed brow. "I want you to know the people I lost, baby. They own the rest of my heart. I have some scrapbooks in my Marine Corps trunk, but I've just never had the guts to pull them out and start looking at them."

"Why?" Alexa gave him a tender look, feeling his heartache as he missed the family he'd loved so much.

With a ragged sigh, Gage looked down and shook his head. "Because I'm afraid if I do, I'll start crying and I'll never stop." He lifted his chin, holding her understanding expression. "Does that make sense?"

"Yes . . . yes, it does, Gage." Alexa smoothed a few short strands away from his temple, aching inside for him. "I can't imagine what I'd do if my family was suddenly taken from me. I'd probably go insane. I rely on all of them so much. Tal, Matt, and I are glued to one another's hips. Oh, I know all families, at least the healthy ones, are very close, too. I just can't imagine myself alone and without my family. I . . . just can't. I don't know how you manage . . ."

"But your Turkish and Greek families are really tight," he said. "I've found in my travels around the world that American families are pretty independent, separated and dispersed from each other. Sometimes they can be a whole coast away from each other. I wouldn't like that. I loved that Mom made sure we were a well-loved, tight-knit family even though Dad was gone overseas on multiple deployments. We did have Skype, and we really looked forward to talking with Dad, hearing his voice. It was like he was reaching out of that video connection and holding me and Jen. We felt his love like he was right there beside us, not half a world away. It was an amazing, magical thing to us kids. Mom said it was our love for one another that made it happen."

"I believe that," Alexa whispered, sliding her hand across his chest. "Well, as soon as I can get myself healed, I truly want to start *our* family, Gage. Not all my dreams are nightmares. Once last week, I woke up and remembered a good dream. I saw me giving birth to this beautiful little golden-haired baby. Funny, because neither of us is blond. I was thinking about that and I remember that earlier that evening, you were talking about Jen and how she always thought her blond hair was too thin and straight."

"Hmm," Gage grinned, cheering up. "I like that you're dreaming of being a mother."

Alexa chewed on her lower lip, her brows drawing down. "I do worry, Gage. I don't want to be like this when I get pregnant. I want to be like I used to be. I don't want to subject a baby to how I'm feeling right now." She met his shadowed eyes, his full attention on her, his arms protecting her, giving her such a sense of peace. The man always had this incredible serenity around him, and she wondered if it was just part of being a sniper. Gage didn't get rattled about anything.

"Well," he soothed, grazing her cheek, "we have time, Alexa. Do I want a family? Yes. But right now isn't the time. You're working to heal from that trauma, and until you feel you're in a quieter space emotionally, I don't think bringing a baby into the world is the smartest thing to do, either."

"But I feel like I should hurry," she confessed hoarsely. "I'm almost thirty. All my life, I've always wanted a family, Gage. My Turkish aunts and uncles do nothing but dream of when we kids will settle down, get married, and have a slew of children they can adore and love. And my Greek cousin, Angelo, and his sweet wife, Maria, have three children of their own. I grew up, Gage, surrounded by tons of relatives in Turkey and Greece when we'd visit during summer vacation."

"That's what I'm saying. Your Turkish and Greek relatives are very, very close as a family."

"And I love it, Gage." Alexa lifted her gaze, melting into his. "You have no idea how badly I want to get off the birth control pills and love you and know we're creating a baby from that love."

Wincing inwardly, Gage felt her conflict and the heartache it brought her. "You're naturally maternal," he whispered, kissing her brow, caressing her cheek, trying to give her some ease from her heart's pain. "And one day, you're going to make an incredible mother, Alexa."

"It's natural for you, too, Gage. You're a father by nature. You're so quiet, gentle, and you don't act like the guys out there who think with what's between their legs."

His mouth curved, and he gave her an amused look. "Now, I have to admit, when I first met you, I *was* thinking with what's between my legs. I couldn't help myself, because you were so alive, so radiant, like blinding sunlight to me. And here you were in the middle of war-torn Afghanistan, so pretty and untouched. The rest of us poor bastards were falling all over ourselves just to feel that sunlight when you'd smile or laugh."

She snorted and playfully elbowed him. "You were *never* like any of those guys at Bagram, Gage. You stood out from them. You were a gentleman when I walked over to the table at the canteen to meet Matt for lunch. You stood up, pulled out my chair, and called me 'ma'am.' You were so courtly compared to those guys slobbering at the bar. Testosterone was so thick in there you could have cut it with a knife."

"You were a ray of sunlight after all the crap

those guys had to face daily," he reminded her, somber, holding her gaze. "You didn't see that, Alexa, but I did. It's like having lived with the stench of blood in your nostrils for a year and suddenly, you step outside and you smell fresh air. It's shocking, dizzying, and freeing."

"And that's what was really happening in that canteen?" Giving him a derisive look, Alexa muttered, "Sorry, but my female senses tell me that it was pure testosterone, all those dudes being horny as hell and wanting a woman. *Any* woman."

Chuckling, he shrugged. "Well, maybe that, too. But at least those animals had good taste." And then he gave her a teasing look. "But I'm the lucky bastard who won your heart."

She leaned up, kissing him for a long, warm moment, her hand resting against his jaw. He smelled of fresh air, sweat, and raw maleness that always made her want to love him once again. As her lips parted from his, she absorbed that feral intensity suddenly coming to his eyes, that hunter in him. "You are so much a better man than I have ever met, Gage. I love you so much I hurt sometimes," she said, and she leaned upward, curving her lips to his mouth, needing that tender contact he always afforded her. Alexa could tell he was monitoring her. She could feel it. A sniper registered thousands of smells, movements, and changes in color in any given second when out on an op. They were human computers that read their surroundings with practiced, detailed ease. He read her. He had from the beginning. Alexa was convinced that because of his amazing abilities, he had often successfully negotiated her and her swinging, abrupt mood changes.

Gage said nothing, but he didn't have to. He closed his arms around her, bringing her against him, holding her close, holding her tight, as if sensing this was what she needed. And it was. Alexa was forever amazed at his eye for detail in the minutia of everyday life, and his ability to winnow out what didn't matter, but knowing unerringly what was important to her.

Sighing, she whispered, "I don't want my anxiety to come back, Gage . . ." and tears pricked her closed lids. Alexa knew it would. She burrowed beneath his chin, clinging to him, inhaling his calming scent. She picked up the slow, solid beat of his heart beneath her opened palm on his chest, wanting to absorb him forever.

"One day," he told her gruffly, kissing her ear, her temple, "it won't be there, Alexa. Becka, your therapist, told you that herself."

"But it makes me crazy. And you're like my whipping post, Gage. You just take my moods, my anger, my lashing out, as if it doesn't hurt you. But I know it does, and I'm so sorry. I don't try to hurt other people. I hate when it happens." She gave him an apologetic look. "When I'm like that, I'm not myself. I'm . . . irrational. I won't listen to anyone. It's driving me crazy, because I can barely control it."

"Hush," he murmured, kissing her cheek, kissing her mouth, hearing the pain and tears in her voice. "It's going to be all right in the long run. You just got out of this trauma a few months ago. You're early in your healing process."

Gage knew Alexa hated taking medication. Becka had tried to give her a sleep med and an antianxiety med, but she'd refused to take them and suffered deeply as a result. Gage wanted to help her, but he was helpless beyond a certain point. "I love you, Alexa. Just hold on to that. Your family loves you, too. And we'll ride this through with you all the way."

Alexa pressed her head against his brow, her arms going around his shoulders. "I just wish it would hurry up and leave me the hell alone. It exhausts me. If I'm not depressed, I'm hyper and manic. I feel like a damned ping pong ball getting batted back and forth, Gage."

He lifted his brow from hers, looking deeply into her anguished hazel eyes. "You'll never be a ping pong ball. You're too pretty." Gage offered her a slight smile, tenderly kissing her, wanting to infuse Alexa with his love, his belief in her working through this trauma. More than anything, as he skimmed his mouth against her lips, easing them open, sliding his tongue between them, tasting her, hearing her moan softly, he wanted to banish the returning anxiety. She quivered, a sign that he was giving her pleasure.

Without a word, he eased Alexa down on the blanket, his arm beneath her neck. She opened her eyes and he saw arousal in them. Leaning down, he slid his other hand beneath her tee, knowing she wasn't wearing a bra. He cupped her breast, watching the nipple become a sharp point against the cotton material. He eased the material upward, revealing it. Watching her, holding her drowsy, hungry gaze, he reached down and closed his lips over that hard bud. Instantly, Alexa moaned, her hips bucking upward, her hand gripping his shoulder, willing him silently to stay and suckle her nipple as shards of fire leaped from there down to her simmering lower body.

This time, he licked it, teased it, and then drew it into his mouth to drive her out of her mind. Gage could chase her anxiety away by loving her. It was medication of another sort. Alexa came unhinged in his arms, her hips urgently pressing against his jeans where his cock twitched and thickened, hungry for her again. Her cries became low and her breath grew ragged as he ruthlessly tugged and suckled on that sweet nipple of hers. He would never cause Alexa pain, at least in loving her, but he could walk her along that very fine edge of pleasure/pain that would bring a woman to a swift orgasm if the man knew how to do it.

"Let's take off your tee," he urged, helping her sit up. "I'm going to love you out of your mind." He saw her give him a shaky look, her hands trembling as she tried to grasp the ends of her tee. With a tender smile, he rasped, "Let me undress you . . ." and he brought the tee over her head, dropping it nearby. Urging her to lie on her back, he opened her shorts and pulled them down. Lastly, he took off her sneakers and socks, mentally photographing her beautiful, sinuous body spread out on the bright green wool blanket. Her auburn hair was thick, glistening, creating a halo about her head and shoulders.

He took off his tee, throwing it aside, opened his jeans and unzipped them. Pushing off the jeans after getting rid of his hiking boots, he came back to Alexa, lying by her side, sliding one arm beneath her neck. As he captured her other nipple with his lips, she cried out, leaning into him, her one hand gripping his shoulder, pulling him closer, feeling his throbbing erection brushing against her rounded belly. At the same time, Gage moved his other hand across her mound, his fingers sliding into her moist folds, knowing she was very close to orgasm once more. In the back of his mind, he knew that by loving her, he could keep the anxiety at bay for another hour or two. As he slid two fingers into her slick, juicy entrance, she cried out, hips powering toward him, wanting more. She clenched, losing her mind to the boiling heat he was creating with his skill. Gasps tore out of her as Gage eased his way into her. She moaned his name, her fingers gripping the short hair near his nape, begging him to alleviate the pressure building up within her.

Gage lifted his lips to the other nipple and he grazed the peak with his teeth. It was just enough pain-pleasure. Almost instantly, she was coming, coming, and screaming. He felt the orgasm hurtle her to a place where nothing, not even memories, could touch her. Opening her thighs, he blanketed her, easing into her tight, wet channel. He lost his mind as she hungrily thrust her hips, pulling him fully into her.

Gage felt his whole body explode with hers. And, in the midst of their passionate union, he gave thanks that he could give the woman he loved a reprieve from the nightmares of her past.

CHAPTER 3

G AGE TRIED TO downplay the concern he felt
for Alexa as he stood near the door of the
Delos Gulfstream jet at Reagan National Airport
near Washington, D.C., a week later. She and her
newly hired assistant, Sarina Elstad, were
boarding the jet. Before they'd left for the airport,
he'd wanted to give Alexa a farewell kiss, but
she'd been cold to him since she'd awakened,
barely speaking to him. Their wonderful time on
the hill above the farmland was now just a dream
from the past. He'd wanted it to last, but knew it
never did. Two days afterward, Alexa had cycled
down into that PTSD pit of high cortisol once
more. It was painful to watch her being tortured
by it, all her emotions distorted and making her
edgy, irritable, and argumentative over nothing.
And that's exactly what had happened at the
office yesterday. Gage didn't want Alexa to go to

Paris because she was still raw and healing. She bull-doggedly forged ahead and told him she was going. Worse? She erupted over dinner at their home when he tried to gently bring it up once again, hoping she would be more reasonable. But that's not what happened.

Miserable, Gage knew he hadn't exactly approached the issue very well himself. He loved Alexa, and he was overprotective of her for a lot of good reasons, but she saw it as suffocating her. That had hurt him deeply. And they were still reeling from that fight. Now, she was cold and distant with him, equally hurt by his words and his trying to get her to stay home and heal. Gage knew Alexa had an undue responsibility to others. It had been bred into her by her global family, who believed in serving those who had less. It was not only a calling, but a duty. And Alexa took her obligation seriously. Sometimes, he felt, far too much. There was a time to fight and a time to stop and heal. She didn't know her own limitations yet, and that's what bothered Gage the most.

The late September sky was cloudy, and it began to rain before dawn. Pulling the sheepskin collar of his leather bombardier jacket up to protect his exposed neck, Gage watched Alexa disappear inside the jet. His heart broke a little more, not wanting to part like this.

He'd tried to talk her into not going to the

sex trafficking conference held in Paris, because he knew she wasn't ready for it. Instead, he'd tried to persuade her to let Sarina go by herself to represent Artemis Security. The Norwegian blonde, a blue-eyed beauty of twenty-eight, was a Ph.D. from Harvard whose whole life had been dedicated to battling sex traffickers, and she had one of the highest profiles in the world, which was why Alexa had hired her for Artemis.

Sarina would be given the job of managing the sex trafficking department under Alexa's Safe House Foundation, a division of Artemis. After Alexa had told Gage one night after dinner that Sarina's sister, Kiara, had been kidnapped at the age of fifteen and forced into sexual servitude, Gage fought his instinctive reaction to go out and find the bastards who'd done it.

Sarina's father was a wealthy shipping magnate in Norway and had spent millions trying to find his youngest daughter. Finally, she'd been spotted by a hired security contractor over the small European country of Malgar, bordered by Macedonia and Albania. Her father recaptured her and brought her home to Oslo, Norway, after five years of enslavement. Kiara had been brainwashed, drugged, and sent to "sex school" to learn how to please her future master. She'd been given a designer sex drug known as Compliance twice a week, just in time for the clients' arrivals. Although she was abused sexually, because of Compliance, she would never have any memory of what had happened. Gage supposed that it was actually a blessing in disguise.

Frowning, Gage turned away, walking back toward the gate as the jet's engines whined to life. In Alexa's case, she had also been given a drug during the physical exam performed by the monsters who had planned to sell her to the highest bidder. Unfortunately, that drug had rendered her body so weak, she couldn't fight back. Her mind, however, was left clear, so the abuse would be held in her memory forever. And to this day, it lived within her, which is how she developed PTSD symptoms.

Sticking his hands into his jacket pockets, Gage turned at the gate. As the jet was given clearance and headed out toward the runway, he lifted his hand to Alexa, whom he saw in one of the small, round windows. She had been so looking forward to this conference. Sarina had brought together a high-powered group of human rights directors, all of whom were passionate about shutting down sex trafficking in their particular country.

The jet slowly trundled away, and Gage felt his concern morph into ice-cold fear. He couldn't get the words or images of Kiara's capture, torture, and brainwashing out of his mind. One of the major sex traffickers in the world was a billionaire named Valdrin Rasari, who made his "legitimate" money in oil, textiles, and steel mills. He hid his dark activities in the country of Malgar, where the government left him alone because of the money he poured into their needy coffers.

Kiara had been kidnapped by Rasari's men, predatory animals walking the streets of nearly every country in the world. They looked for girls and boys as young as age twelve, kidnapping them right off the streets. The victims were then brought to Malgar, to a town called Lugina Pisha, or Pine Tree, where Rasari had his compound.

Gage hunched his shoulders, turned, and walked through the guarded gate. Outside was his gray Kia SUV. Had it only been a week ago that he and Alexa had taken that unforgettable hike and made love to one another in the woods?

Concerned that Alexa was diving into this lurid, monstrous business too fast, Gage had talked with Becka yesterday, who had cautioned Alexa not to go to the conference; she agreed with Gage that she wasn't emotionally prepared for it.

Gage climbed into the SUV, rain dripping off his face. Shutting the door, he watched as the jet rolled along the runway toward a distant takeoff point. Alexa was in a downswing in her PTSD cycle, that was clear, and Gage couldn't reason with her when she became emotional and at times, almost hysterical.

Last night, Alexa had exploded angrily at him, telling him she wanted to sleep alone and that he could sleep on the couch. Damn it, he hated when she was at the mercy of a hormone known as cortisol.

Feeling hurt and upset, he'd barely slept last night out on the couch. Gage didn't blame Alexa for her reaction to his attempt to keep her safe. He was becoming familiar with the stages of her suffering. Now she needed to prove to herself that she still had the courage to confront her own traumatic experience.

Of course, Alexa didn't need to prove anything to him or anyone else. Gage wearily moved his fingers through his dark, rain-soaked hair, started the Kia, turned on the wiper blades, and watched for the Delos jet to safely take off.

His mind swung back to Valdrin Rasari. The man was a huge black hole. Kiara had been the most extensive source of information about him and his infamous compound. Until her, no one had ever escaped from it, and lived to provide such lurid testimony.

The compound had been hidden in a narrow valley covered with pine trees, mountains ringing three sides of it, and a lake on the fourth side. Kiara had said that the compound was really a breeding facility. Men called "breeders" impregnated the women, known as "broodmares." The children produced were cruelly taken from their sex slave mothers at three months old. Those children were already sold and sent to their respective parents in some other part of the world. At that time, a broodmare would be bred again to have another child by a selected breeder.

Gage could hardly believe what he had heard. He was equally stunned by the complex infrastructure Rasari had created.

Malgar was a third world country into which Rasari poured billions. The government, as far as he was concerned, was merely a puppet whose strings the sick monster pulled. He had created his evil facilities without government oversight, and because Malgar was not in the European Union, it answered to no one.

Women like Kiara, then in her teens, were the most highly prized and sought after on the street. They were physically mature and able to provide sexual services. They were usually beautiful and still young enough to be brainwashed, threatened, and forced into sexual slavery. Gage could barely stand hearing about what these young children were put through. His heart ached for all of them.

Wiping his face, he knew why he couldn't get through to Alexa. She was driven and committed to her work, and he agreed with Tal, her big sister, that this trip would be a distraction for Alexa. She was running away from her trauma, trying to bury it beneath the traumas of others, which was somehow easier to deal with.

Jesus, what a mess. Alexa was in free fall, heading for a darker place if she didn't pull out of this dive. The conference would traumatize her even more, he was sure of that.

The jet taking her to Paris, its yellow and red stripes proclaiming its identity, took off, disappearing into the rainy gray sky. Frowning, Gage drove out of the parking lot. This was one miserable day. He should have kissed Alexa goodbye, even though she was pissed as hell at him. He should have told her he loved her. But he'd done neither. And she'd been icy and withdrawn, her glare accusatory, as if he weren't supporting her when she needed him to be there for her. He'd had no intention of forcing himself upon her, but regrets were always a mean son of a bitch.

VALDRIN RASARI TOOK one last look in the mirror of the Fontainebleau Hotel, only blocks from the famed Eiffel Tower. He smiled coldly into the full-length gold framed mirror. His mouth curved even more at the irony that he, one of the major sex traffickers in the world, would be a wolf in sheep's clothing at this conference on sex slavery. He could easily travel the world in disguise with forged passports. Right now, fifty countries had him on their no-fly list. Only third world countries were open to him buying the best children from parents who were starving. *Sell me your child, and you will live to put food on the table for a year for the rest of your family. It's a good trade.*

Tonight, at the cocktail party in the huge chandelier ballroom downstairs, no one would recognize him. At six feet tall, muscular without being muscle-bound, he would carry a cane, under the guise of Dr. Analius Revig from the University of Oslo. His injury was from a "skiing accident" in his twenties, of course. Today, his short black hair was dyed gray, and his square-jawed face now sported a sporty gray mustache. His brown eyes had blue contacts over them, covered further by a pair of fashionable wire-rim glasses. After all, he was pretending to be a sixty-five-year-old man . . .

Since his alter ego was a professor at the University of Oslo, he dressed in a fashionable brown wool sport coat and black wool trousers. Valdrin was exceedingly sensitive to anything touching his flesh, so beneath the black trousers he wore the world's finest silk boxer shorts. Never mind that they cost a thousand dollars— they were worth it. His cock was long, thick, and super-sensitive to touch or material covering it. Under the elegant coat, he wore a white cotton shirt that had been ironed to perfection; it gave him a professorial look. He wore a black bow tie that was in keeping with the look he desired.

He was looking forward to prowling the huge gathering, eavesdropping, and seeing who was there. Valdrin took great enjoyment in being undercover. He spoke six different languages, Norwegian being one of them. Placing his old leather wallet into his coat pocket and his passport in an inner pocket, he adopted the proper slump and slight lean to the right, his cane in his left hand. Fortunately, he had one of those nondescript faces that no one would ever recognize. In fact, he had destroyed any photos of himself for the last thirty of his forty-five years. No one really knew who the monstrous Rasari was or how he looked, even while he was on every country's radar.

He left his bodyguards behind, a door between the sumptuous rooms. They were handlers from the compound who also looked nondescript, nothing like the usual hulking guards. He smiled, ruffling his hair so it looked like an older person's hair. Perfecting his slump to the right and engaging a proper limp, he walked around the huge suite until he felt comfortable with his disguise.

The ballroom was packed with men in black tuxedos and women in tasteful European gowns or pantsuits, but Valdrin didn't worry about his appearance. As a university professor, he would be easily forgiven for such fashion oversight. He limped slowly, skirting the outside of the gathering. Wine was flowing, but not much hard liquor. He knew this group quite well, because he was their number one focus among the world's most loathed sex traffickers. He smiled faintly, keeping his head bent slightly as he looked up through his false bushy gray eyebrows.

A redheaded woman with a blond woman beside her caught his attention. Moving out of the walkway, he leaned casually against the heavily brocaded gold wallpaper and watched. Who was this woman? He'd not seen her before. Over the years, Valdrin had learned and committed to his impeccable memory all the major leaders in the human rights movement. This woman was new. Some of his interest was doused as he saw the blonde beside her was none other than Sarina Elstad. His lips twitched, remembering how lush and sexually hungry her sweet little sister, Kiara, had been. For two years, she had been his favorite BDSM sub—and what a fine sub she had been. At first, she'd fought him, but he would give her the drug Compliance and watch her turn from fiery fighter to a whimpering, sexually starved woman who would do anything to attain an orgasm.

One of the nice side effects of Compliance was that a woman's womb began to cramp, as if she were having cramps during her menstrual period. The gnawing, edgy pain was actually the body hormonally wanting to be bred so a woman could become fertile.

Kiara had become pregnant four times in those two years. And each time, Valdrin had given her a pill for her to abort the fetus, after which she would be understandably sore and tender for the next few days. He never wore a condom when one of his personal sex slaves was on Compliance. In fact, he disdained condoms completely. They robbed a man of exquisite sensations and pleasures.

Hatred mixed with desire for Kiara. Her sister, Sarina, was now one of the most influential women on earth, giving passionate speeches about the effects of sexual slavery upon men and women. She used her anger over her sister's capture and consequent imprisonment well. Valdrin often wondered just how much Kiara remembered of his BDSM sessions with her. There was no "safe word" for her. He did as he pleased to her, wreaking pain and pleasure upon her.

When Kiara was on Compliance, she had loved the pain, as it heightened her sexual experiences times ten. But when he didn't use it, she would scream. He hated that!

As he watched Sarina smile, shake hands, and talk to the eager attendees surrounding her, Valdrin was reminded of Kiara, who eventually broke beneath his relentless weekly BDSM sessions. He found she actually surrendered more easily without Compliance. He supposed it was the pain threshold that had broken her most quickly. Kiara had been a fighter, and he preferred a woman who fought back. They always lost, of course, but their struggles boosted his sexual pleasure.

Someone like Kiara, who had been kidnapped while riding her bike from school, was unskilled, untrained, and inept. Slaves like that were far more volatile and rebellious, always fighting and trying to escape. He had clients who liked them that way, as he did.

Valdrin smiled even more, watching the redhead. She was probably in her late twenties, curvy, nice looking in that purple sheath she wore. It wasn't provocative, but he sometimes liked to role play with his sex slaves, dress them up and then undress them. He'd like to undress this redhead. She had fine, flawless, white skin. When she partially turned his way, he saw that she was a true beauty.

Instinctively, Valdrin placed her in the "natural woman" category—the outdoorsy type. Her breasts were a nice size, probably 34Bs, and she was fluid and graceful as she moved toward a table close to where he was standing.

As she drew closer, he nearly lost his suave control, which was unusual. He saw on the woman's name tag that she was Alexa Culver. *THE Culvers?* His heart started to beat harder. His gaze narrowed to the words beneath her name: Delos Charities. It felt as if the wind had been torn out of his chest for a moment. Valdrin suddenly moved and caught her in a sideswipe. He grunted, falling hard to his knees, cane flying out of his hand.

Alexa gave a cry as she bumped into the older man. She was horrified that she hadn't seen him and had accidentally knocked him down. What was wrong with her? Feeling guilty, she quickly righted herself, flying to his side, kneeling down beside him. He was on his hands and knees, looking as if he were shaken. She placed her arm across his shoulders, her hand on his right arm. "Oh, I'm so sorry. Are you hurt? This was all my fault. I wasn't watching where I was going!"

Valdrin smiled and shook his head. "No . . . no, my dear . . . I will be all right. Just give an old man a moment." He twisted, looking directly into her huge hazel eyes fraught with apology and anxiety. Groaning, and not from pain, his cock swelled swiftly. She had lips that were sheer perfection. Valdrin snapped himself out of his sexual fantasies and sat up slowly, leaning back on his heels. Someone else came over, a man, and offered to help him up. He allowed him to do just that as Alexa Culver picked up his cane.

"Are you sure you're all right?" She peered at his suit coat and looked at the name tag on it. "Doctor Revig?" Pressing the cane into his hand, she whispered, "I'm so very, very sorry."

"Tut-tut. Call me Analius." He turned and thanked the gentleman who had helped him to stand, then nodded in a courtly manner and walked away, feeling Alexa's long, slender hand around his arm, steadying him.

"Would you be so kind as to help me back to my hotel room? I'm afraid my one knee feels very weak." He saw her expression grow crushed over his admittance of being injured. It always amazed him how gullible people were. He was a wolf, and she was the sheep in his sights. A thrill went through him as she nodded her head.

"Of course, Dr. Revig. It's the least I can do. Are you sure you don't need me to get the house doctor, or a wheelchair?"

"No, no," he said, leaning a bit on her arm, limping. "You will be my house doctor, my dear Ms. Culver."

"Oh please, call me Alexa. I just feel so terrible about this. I see on your nametag that you have a Ph.D. in human rights from the University of Oslo."

He hobbled expertly, and they left the ballroom. At the bank of elevators, he pressed the tenth-floor button. "Yes, but I am also an international lawyer by trade, Alexa."

Alexa helped him into the elevator. "Is this your first conference with human rights?"

"Oh," he chortled. "No, no, my dear. I have been involved in this all my life." He laughed to himself, enjoying the charade, seeing how stupid and accepting she was. He knew a lot about the Culver family, but had only a photo of each of the children when they were in the military.

Alexa was a combat pilot flying the A-10, known as the Warthog. He was having a tough time reconciling the shaky, unsure woman before him with the image of a combat pilot. The two did not mix. *Interesting.* She captivated him. She would be someone he'd choose for his BDSM group. Although she wasn't trained, he would look forward to training her. Because once he got her to his room, he would drug her and call his nearby bodyguards, and they would leave the hotel immediately, flying her back to Malgar.

Wait until his friend, Zakir Sharan, found out he'd stumbled upon one of the Culver children! He was sure Zakir would try and buy her off him, hell-bent on torturing any of the Culver children for the death of his two beloved sons, Raastagar and Sidiq. Matt Culver had also murdered his son, Agnon, as well. Both Zakir and Valdrin had a blood revenge against the family, as well as Delos Charities in general. No, he would keep Alexa Culver for himself and extract his own kind of revenge against her. He smiled to himself.

After he grew weary or bored with getting his revenge, if she survived, Valdrin would sell her to his friend, Zakir. He was sure Alexa would not survive at Zakir's hands very long. Valdrin knew Alexa was not responsible for killing Zakir's sons, but that didn't matter. He could still slyly use her to make the Culver family suffer for years to come.

No, he would not kill Alexa Culver. Instead, he would, over time and with drugs, brainwash her, make her compliant to his BDSM demands, and teach her to be subservient to him, the dominator. And of course, while he was taming her into submission, videos would be taken of her, and those tapes would find their way onto Robert and Dilara's computers. His revenge was going to be painful and ongoing for the Culver family.

He almost laughed over his plan. Alexa would become like the rest of the sex slaves at the compound. She would surrender to him and become subservient, never even thinking of escaping or wanting to leave. She would spend the rest of her life with him, until he either grew tired of her or had extracted the maximum amount of vengeance upon the Culver family.

Valdrin and Alexa walked down the carpeted hall to his suite. As he slowly handed her the card to open the door, he smiled pleasantly. "My knee feels a bit better."

"That's good!" she said, relief in her voice as she opened the white door surrounded by gold, ornate trim.

Valdrin liked her maternal caregiving. He might even, after a few years, have her bred to one of his superior breeder studs. He even entertained the thought of impregnating her himself so she would carry his child. Now wouldn't that be sweet revenge against the Culvers—to make monthly videos showing Alexa being impregnated by him until she conceived! And then monthly updates showing her swelling belly, culminating with actual videos of the birth of his son coming out of her.

Ah! A thrill arced through Valdrin. To him, that would be the ultimate revenge. And the Culver family would never see their daughter again. Yes, he liked that idea quite a bit. Zakir would be angry, but so what? He would have a son born from his archenemy, whom he could teach how sex and pleasure were a natural, daily occurrence and to be acted upon, just as his mother had done with him.

GAGE WAS AT his desk at Artemis, having just come inside when his landline phone rang. He'd had lunch outside at a group of picnic tables beneath some trees that had nearly lost all their leaves. Tal and Matt had joined him, and they had discussed their concerns and worries for Alexa. They had sought Gage out to ask him questions about what they could do to support and help her through this rough period in her healing process. Tal and Matt wanted to speak further with him, following him to his office. Gage had just shut the door to his office and when the phone rang.

"Hunter here," he said, standing again.

"Gage Hunter?" The voice sounded halting, tremulous, riddled with anxiety.

He frowned. "Sarina? Is that you?"

"Yes, it's Sarina. Gage, Alexa was kidnapped! Thank God, the French gendarmes quickly found out where she was located, and she's safe. It was Valdrin Rasari!"

His heart leaped, and he pressed a button on the phone. "Sarina, Tal and Matt are here with me. Tell us what happened. Is Alexa all right?" He knew the name Valdrin Rasari, and his gut clenched into a painful, tight fist. Matt and Tal were instantly on their feet, standing close to the desk as Sarina breathlessly told them what happened.

"Yes, Alexa is going to be all right. They have taken her by ambulance to a nearby hospital, which is where I'm calling from. The doctor later came back and said she'd been given a drug. He called it a date rape drug. But when the police broke into Valdrin's suite, she was fully dressed and appeared untouched. Alexa is still coming out of the drug state and isn't fully coherent yet. When she is, I'll get her to call you."

"Then," Gage rasped, "she wasn't raped?" He hated even saying the word, bitterness coating the inside of his mouth.

"The woman doctor who is caring for Alexa has talked to her. She has no memory of being touched at all, but of course, with a date rape drug, you usually have no memory. Alexa consented to an exam, and the doctor said there is no evidence of penetration. She thinks that the man who did this had just given it to her and was waiting for the drug to take full effect before he acted."

Relief plunged through Gage. He wiped his face, sitting down, his knees suddenly weakening. "Thank God," he whispered. Looking up, he saw the relief on Tal and Matt's grim faces. Both had paled, and he was sure he didn't look very good himself. "But she's going to be okay?" He couldn't help but ask it again.

"Yes, the doctor found no marks, no bruises, or anything on Alexa."

Tal made a signal to Gage.

"Hold on, Tal wants to speak. Matt is also here, Sarina."

Gage choked on bile and looked away as Tal launched into details about getting Alexa transferred from the hospital to the Delos company jet at the DeGaulle Airport. Matt came around the desk and gripped his shoulder, giving him a concerned look. Nausea rolled through Gage. His mind whirled with the implications of this attack on Alexa. There was a fatwa out on the three Culver children by Zakir Sharan. But Sarina had said this was Valdrin Rasari? How did that monster get into that hotel? How?

Tal nodded when she finished speaking to Sarina. "Okay, once you find out when Alexa can travel, let's get her to the Delos jet and get her home. After that, I think everyone will rest a little easier."

"I agree," Sarina said. "I just feel so sorry for Alexa. She was semiconscious and seemed to realize what had happened to her. This is just awful, Tal. She's just trying to come out of that first sexual assault. Now this. I . . . I'm sorry I didn't go with her. The police think it was Valdrin Rasari. He's known to go into disguise, fooling everyone."

Matt stepped forward, hands on his hips. "Sarina? Matt here. Do you think Valdrin Rasari recognized Alexa as being a Culver?"

"I-I don't know. Of course, we all wore name badges at that conference. He could have read it and realized who she was. Maybe we can find out when Alexa gets home?"

Matt's mouth twisted, and he glanced over at Tal. "We've suspected that Zakir Sharan and

Valdrin Rasari knew one another. That's why I asked. It could be that Rasari knew Alexa would be at this conference and came in disguise to kidnap her, drug her, and take her somewhere. Maybe to Pakistan or Malgar."

Gage sat there hearing the heaviness in Matt's voice, seeing the concern in his golden-brown eyes. Tal stepped over, protectively settling her hand on her younger brother's tense broad shoulder.

Gage felt gutted. He was both relieved and totally bewildered. What kind of emotional shape was Alexa in? What did she remember, if anything?

"Tell us how it happened," Matt said to Sarina.

"I saw Alexa go toward the wine table, and she accidentally bumped into an older gentleman. He fell and she helped him up, very apologetically. I saw her help him to his feet. He was older, maybe sixty-five or so, gray-haired, with a cane. I didn't recognize him, and I know most of the people in human rights and sex trafficking who attend these conferences. That bothered me, so I dug out my cell phone and put a call in to Alexa.

"She said she was in Dr. Analius Revig's suite at the hotel, helping him get settled because he'd wrenched his knee in that fall. She told me he was a professor of human rights at University of Oslo. That set off alarms in me, because I am on the staff of the Human Rights Department at the university, and I did not recognize his name. I had a horrible feeling and followed my gut, calling the hotel police, and then they called in the French gendarmes."

"How long between Alexa leaving the ball-room and when the gendarmes broke into the suite?" Tal demanded, scowling.

"Probably fifteen minutes maximum."

Gage breathed heavily. That wasn't enough time to drug and rape a person, was it? He knew so little of sex trafficking, the drugs, and the monsters who were the worst kind of predators in the world. He saw Matt's face show relief. Tal's did, too.

"In your opinion," Tal asked, "is that enough time to drug a victim and then rape her?"

"No. Depending upon the dosage of such a drug," Sarina said, "it takes at least twenty minutes to actually take effect and render the victim unconscious."

"When the gendarmes broke into that room and found Alexa," Matt asked, "was she uncon-scious?"

"No. I was there. She was still awake. Not very coherent, quite confused, but not uncon-scious."

"Did you apprehend those who did this to her?" Tal demanded.

"No, he slipped into the next room and escaped the gendarmes. There were three men, and they ran for the exit stairs and got away."

Matt muttered a curse, his hands flexing into fists. Tal nodded, her eyes flashing with anger.

"Let's just get her home," Tal ordered. "I'm calling in two of our security contractors who work the Paris area. I'll have them there at Alexa's hospital room within an hour." She picked up her cell phone, found the addresses, and quickly gave the two men's names. "At no time," she warned Sarina in a dark voice, "is Alexa to be out of sight of our Artemis team. Is that understood? We don't know who tried to kidnap her, even though your suspicions may be well founded."

"Oh," Sarina said. "I fully agree with your plan, Tal. It's a good one. Right now, two gendarmes are standing guard outside her hospital room door. I'll tell them what will be happening so they know to expect these two Artemis contractors."

"Good idea," Tal said. "But I'll have Matt call them and get them up to speed, probably in another hour. Will Alexa be more coherent then?"

"For sure. I know the doctor gave her an IV full of medication to wash whatever they gave her out of her bloodstream faster. The doctor also took blood samples, so she'll know what drug Alexa was given as well."

"Absolutely," Tal said. "Have that doctor send Becka, our therapist, the results here at Artemis, okay?"

"Of course. Well, listen, I'm going to go—there are two French detectives coming down the hall toward me. They might have more information. If there is, I'll call you immediately, Tal."

"Do that," she growled, scowling.

Tal looked at Matt and Gage after hanging up. "The good news is Alexa was rescued and she wasn't raped. The bad news is that this is happening to her again in a very short space of time. Dammit, anyway!"

CHAPTER 4

G AGE TRIED TO contain his emotions as he
stood with the Culver family at Reagan
National Airport. It was late afternoon, chilly, but
this time the skies were clear. The group stood
huddled together near a ten-foot-tall cyclone
fence. The Delos jet had just landed, and Alexa
was on it.

Dilara, her mother, was nervously shifting
from one foot to the other, her leather-gloved
hands clasped against her heart, her gaze pinned
on the jet as it came to a stop. Alexa's father,
General Robert Culver, had been at the Pentagon
and rushed over from his office, still in uniform.
Now he stood with his arm around his distraught
wife's shoulders.

His eldest daughter, Tal, stood back, letting
her parents be the first to greet Alexa as she came
down the ramp. Alexa's twin, Matt, was still at

Artemis handling an overseas emergency.

Gage was impatient to see Alexa, but loved and respected how close her family was. He also knew how upset they were over what had just happened to her. As Alexa descended the steps of the plane, Gage anxiously scanned her pale face for clues to her condition. Dilara, unable to hold back, ran toward her daughter as Alexa stepped onto the tarmac, then burst into tears of relief, gripping her youngest daughter close. Robert Culver enfolded both of them into his large embrace.

Tal exchanged a look with Gage, her face impassive. "Give them a moment," she told him. "This is a shock to my parents, as well as to Alexa."

"To all of us. I understand," Gage rasped, standing next to her. His hands were thrust deep in the pockets of his leather jacket. He saw the deep shadows, the shame, and humiliation written in Alexa's expression. She looked fragile, and Tal had warned him that it would take at least forty-eight hours for the drugs to leave her system. He could feel Tal, the eldest of the three siblings, tightly reining in her emotions, too.

Dilara's sobs tore at him, because Gage also felt like crying with relief. But no one yet knew the full story of what had happened to Alexa. Sarina had stayed behind, working with the Paris gendarmes and detectives as they tried to find her kidnappers. Alexa had given Tal all the information she could, but it was spotty at best.

Gage held himself away from the close family as Alexa finally eased out of her mother's arms. She hugged her father, then turned and walked over to Tal, hugging her. Gage didn't mind if he was last, because the importance of family was the best foundation a person could have. He knew that better than anyone.

Alexa lifted her tear-stained face from Tal's shoulder and moved toward Gage, seeing that he was wearing his sniper game face. But even with the drug creating chaos in her system, she could feel his love surrounding her as she walked toward him. He opened his arms, giving her a faint, welcoming smile.

"Oh, Gage," Alexa whispered, her voice breaking as he swept her into his strong, loving embrace. Her heart was pounding with relief and excitement. God, she felt so much love for this man! She buried her face against his leather jacket, breaking into a fresh torrent of tears.

"You're safe now, baby," he said gruffly against her ear, kissing her temple, her damp cheek, and finally, her moist lips. She whispered his name as she clung to him, his mouth sweeping gently across hers. Gage was warm, solid, and steady, unlike her. Eagerly, she kissed him, needing him more than anyone else.

"I love you," he rasped against her lips, looking deep into her eyes. "We'll get through this together . . ."

ALEXA WAS NEVER so glad to be home. She loved their 1850s farmhouse and the antiques they'd bought for it. It made her feel warm and safe. Gage came over, wrapping her in a colorful afghan that her mother had knitted for her as a child. Its shades of green, yellow, and brown matched the color of Alexa's beautiful eyes. She gave him a look of thanks, lying on the couch, her head on a pillow, eyes half closed, clearly exhausted.

"I'm glad we're home," she whispered as he sat beside her, tucking the afghan around her lower body.

"You're completely stressed out," Gage said tenderly, noting the dark smudges beneath her eyes. "What can I do for you, baby?"

She reached out, gripping his hand. "Just this . . . you . . . our home, Gage," she choked, tears streaming from her eyes. "I-I thought I'd never see you again . . ." She was in so much pain, so incredibly humiliated by what had happened. She should have listened to Gage. He didn't want her to go to Paris. Nor did her family. Worse, she and Gage had a terrible fight the night before she left, and she hadn't even kissed him goodbye.

"Listen," he said gently, holding her damp fingers. "You are the victim in all of this, Alexa. Stop looking so ashamed of what happened. You didn't know this guy from Adam. He completely fooled you. He fooled everyone. You just happened to be at the wrong place at the wrong time."

"N-no, that's not true, Gage," she cried softly. "When I was in his suite, and after I'd unknowingly drank the drugged orange juice he offered me, he changed."

"What do you mean?"

"After I helped him to his room, I was sitting at the table, and he offered me orange juice. I thanked him and had a bit. Then, about ten minutes later, the room was blurry, and I felt dizzy. He saw it immediately, and the smile he gave me changed from an old man's smile to one from a much younger man."

"Did he tell you his real name?" Gage probed.

"Yes, he told me." She wiped her hand nervously across her brow. "I recognized the name, Valdrin Rasari, and began to panic. I could see now that he was in disguise." She shivered. "It was awful, Gage . . . awful. I felt the worst sense of doom, like I was going to die."

Gage continued, asking his questions in a soft, gentle voice. "Did he touch you, Alexa?" It hurt to even ask the question, but he knew had to know.

Alexa didn't reply, instead shooting him a shamed look. "Everyone in the sex trafficking world knows who he is. And I fell for the oldest trick in the world!"

He sat watching her, assessing every halting word she spoke. "What happened then?"

"H-he told me what he was going to do with me, now that I was drugged. He told me in another ten minutes I would go unconscious. He had his men in the room next door, waiting to take me down an elevator to a nearby car. He said they would fly me to Malgar, to what he called his 'compound.'"

She touched his hand. "I can only remember some sketchy things, Gage, but my memory is coming back to me. I told the gendarmes what I remembered at the time, after they rescued me. Now I'm starting to remember more."

"You're still under the drug's influence, baby. It only makes sense you'd start remembering more as it leaves your system." He dried her tears with his thumbs, a gesture she'd grown to love. They already had so many tears between them . . .

How badly he wanted to scoop her up, put her on his lap, and hold her. Now she was gripping the edges of her afghan, much like a child might grip a beloved security blanket.

"He told me he was going to keep me alive

so I could be his personal sub."

"'Sub' as in BDSM talk?"

Giving a jerky nod, she said, "Yes. He said BDSM. He said he couldn't live without a daily session with one of his well-trained sex slaves, and I would become one of them." She shivered, pulling the afghan up over her breasts. "I was sitting there, unable to move to escape, listening to him tell me that he was disappointed it was me he'd found, because he really wanted Tal or Matt. But he thought Zakir Sharan would be very pleased that he at least had captured one of the Culver children."

Gage nodded. "Because Sharan swore blood revenge and placed a fatwa against Tal and Matt after they killed his two sons."

"Yes," she confirmed. "And he said that his good friend, Zakir, would probably send me to Pakistan. Rasari laughed, like it was a private joke. I was so dizzy by that time I couldn't speak or think straight. I felt terror, but I couldn't scream for help or move. It was a horrible feeling, Gage."

"But was Rasari telling you he was taking you to his country as his prisoner?" Gage tried to keep his voice low and calm, though he felt anything but. He had to push down his desire to hunt this man down and kill him.

What Rasari had been about to do to Alexa made his stomach knot. If Alexa hadn't been saved, she would have again been tortured by this sociopathic monster. The man didn't feel emotions, remorse, or empathy with other human beings. Receiving pleasure, in his case, was always accompanied by another person's pain and humiliation. He lived for those moments and had built his life around achieving them whenever the urge overtook him.

"What else do you remember him saying to you?" he asked, squeezing her fingers for reassurance. He needed more details before making any moves.

"He said he was going to take me to his compound in Malgar and instruct me in BDSM. I would be taught how to be subservient to him. He said—and this is horrible, Gage—that he would have one of the other slaves take videos of each lesson he'd teach me. I would be kept naked, and each time the session ended, he'd send it to my parents, post it on YouTube, and on other video channels on the Internet." She squeezed her eyes shut, shaking her head. "I-I just can't imagine what that would do to them . . . honest to God, I can't. It would be the worst form of torture to my family . . . the worst . . ."

Grimly, Gage absorbed what she was saying, revealing only his calm, steady exterior, his game face. He smoothed her hair, trying to comfort her. "I can't either, baby. I really can't."

She grimaced, looking down at her tightly

clasped hands. "It gets worse, Gage. I remember now that he promised that once he taught me how to be a good sub, he would get me pregnant. Then he'd take monthly videos of me as the baby grew inside me. When the baby was born, he'd videotape the birth and send that to my family, too. He said the child would be raised by him. At three months, he would take the baby from me and send me to Zakir Sharan. He said it was more than likely that Zakir would behead me shortly after my arrival. He'd take videos of my throat being cut and put the video out on the Internet."

Gage swallowed heavily several times, forcing down his desire to retch. Right now, Alexa needed him to be strong. She was already an emotional wreck from the near kidnapping. "Did you tell the French detectives this?"

Shaking her head miserably, she stole a look over at him. "No . . . as I said, more and more of the conversation is coming back in bits and pieces as the drug wears off." Alexa looked distressed as she plunged on. "Gage, I have to tell my father and Tal that the whole family is under this blood revenge by Sharan and Rasari. These evil men are the best of friends. Sharan is a sex trafficker, but Rasari is far worse."

"What do you mean?"

"H-he proudly told me that at his compound in Malgar he has three-story, dormitory-like buildings on his estate. Inside them are five hundred 'broodmares,' sex slaves who were either born on the estate and raised there, or kidnapped as children off city streets from around the world. He boasted of having the finest geneticists in the world working there for him. These broodmares were genetically altered and bred by what he called 'super stallions,' male slaves who also had spliced genes to produce superior sex slaves. They bred these women once a year, each to genetically match a specific stallion who would impregnate her. If they were running low on blond children—in high demand on the slave market—his scientists would pair the right broodmare with the right super stallion. The resulting baby would have blond hair."

"My God," Gage breathed, staring at her unbelievingly.

"There's more, and it's so unbelievable and sick that I remember wanting to vomit as he told me. He was actually proud of what he was doing—bragging that the resulting babies born from the broodmare spent the first three months on their mother's breast. Then they were taken from them and given to a set of parents who had ordered that particular baby. He said he made millions of dollars that way. That his whole compound was about creating designer babies. Rasari said he could never keep up with the global demand, but it had made him a billionaire over the last decade."

Gage stared at her. "Does anyone else know what this monster is doing?"

"I don't know. I need to talk with Sarina about it. She would know, possibly. Rasari is so private that the world knows little of who or what he is."

"If there is anyone who should be taken out permanently," Gage said, "it's this sick, predatory bastard." He struggled to keep his emotions in check. Gage loved children. As worldly as he was, he couldn't even begin to contemplate what was being done to them at such a young age. And women being raped yearly; impregnated to create a designer baby. It was insane!

"I sat there feeling like a puppet with sawdust in my arms and legs, thinking the same thing. The drug he gave me intensified my feelings times ten, so I was filled with terror and revulsion."

"Can't anyone take this monster down?" Gage asked, amazed that it hadn't already been done.

Shaking her head, Alexa said, "No. Sarina said Malgar's government protects him, and it doesn't have international agreements with certain first world countries that would appre-hend him. The only countries Malgar has agreements with are in Asia and Africa, third world countries, he said, where he gets the bulk of his child slaves. Rasari was very proud of the fact that he had global immunity and would never be identified or caught. No one dares bother the compound; he is free to do whatever he wants there. That government turns a blind eye."

Gage shook his head, giving her a grim look. "Sarina is coming back in a few days. Maybe if you sit down with her, you'll remember more. On the plus side, will all this information help the international community act against him?"

"It should," Alexa said wearily. "I remember sitting there thinking that my life would be an ongoing nightmare, one I wouldn't survive. You should have seen the look in Rasari's eyes. They were dead, Gage. They only lit up when he described what he was going to do to me." She wrapped her arms round herself in a childlike, protective gesture.

"Come here," Gage offered, coaxing Alexa against him. He held her tight, her head tucked in beneath his strong chin, feeling her melt against him. At least she still trusted him, no matter what had happened.

He still didn't know if Rasari had touched her in any way, but he realized Alexa was stressed enough without pursuing the matter. In time, he knew she'd share everything. The only problem was, could he handle it?

ONE WEEK LATER, the entire Culver family and their spouses met in a mission planning room at Artemis Security. Gage had supported Alexa's desire to write down all her memories from her capture. Sarina Elstad, who sat at her left elbow, had helped Alexa gather the information, and then compared Alexa's notes with those of her sister, Kiara. Although Kiara rarely spoke, when she did, Sarina recorded everything she said.

When Alexa and Sarina shared their information with the family, the listeners were at first keenly interested. Their expressions changed to deep concern, ending with stark fear by the time the women had finished their reports. Fortunately, the family had decided to videotape the session. They would send copies to the Turkish and Greek sides of their family, because Zakir Sharan had included on his revenge list, every member of the family, not just the Culvers. That meant all the children of Alexa's aunts and uncles, as well as their cousin Angelo and his wife Maria's children in Greece, were on the hit list.

Dilara dabbed her eyes with her linen hand-kerchief. She sat beside Robert at the other end of the large tiger maple table. "What are we going to do?" she asked, clearly disturbed. Usually cool and calm, she was now grappling with the fact that they had not yet come up with a plan to deal with this situation.

Robert, sensing her fragility, said, "Look. Tal

killed Raastagar less than a year ago, and Matt took out Sidiq, Sharan's other son after that. Agnon Rasari was killed at the same time as Sidiq because he was being taught the sex trade business. To date, no one in any of our far-flung family has been targeted." He looked over at his youngest daughter. "And the only reason Alexa was taken was that she was at the wrong place at the wrong time. I agree with Sarina on this one. Rasari has a history of wearing disguises so he can get around Europe. He may have heard of that human rights conference and went to Paris for the pure hell of it. He's a sociopath, and he feels invulnerable. He may have seen Alexa's name tag, but there aren't that many photos of the three Culver children floating around. I think her name tag alerted him."

Tal scowled and sat up in the chair, resting her elbows on the table, sending her father a concerned look. "Even if Alexa was in the wrong place, Rasari caught one of us—and it was easy! That's what's important here. He's got a taste of success, and my bet is he's going to come after more."

Matt, who sat opposite Tal, said, "I agree. I'm sure he's told Sharan all about it, and if nothing else, it will reignite his desire to try and kidnap as many of us as he can. And he has the money and resources to do it. He's worth forty billion dollars. He can hire anyone he wants."

Tal nodded. "There are several procedures that we need to implement immediately. First, are any of us committed to going to a conference of any kind? If so, we don't use our real names any longer; we go under an assumed name, if we go at all. Many of these human rights conferences are videotaped, or have streaming video that can be watched here at Artemis. We can have the tapes sent here to view them, keeping us protected. Second, every family member needs to be brought up to speed. I don't put it past either of these monsters to go after the parents of these children, so the villas they live in must get security upgrades ASAP."

Matt nodded slowly. "Right. The children of the Kemel and Mykonos families are all adults now, and they all have careers. They live all over the world, and each one is going to need a security detail of some kind. They're all at risk."

"My God, this is overwhelming!" Dilara said, her voice strained.

"Yes," Tal muttered. "It is. But it's not impossible. We can do this, Mom."

"The world is a very small place today," Robert told his wife, sliding his arm around her shoulders. "Anyone with money can have a global reach, whether we like it or not."

Dilara looked around slowly at all her children. "I want you all safe. That's the most important thing in the world to me."

Gage heard her voice tremble—she was a mother first, an executive second. Although her children were all grown, she needed to protect them. Alexa had already had two incidents of being overpowered: once in Afghanistan before she was rescued by Gage, and now in Paris. This was as real as it got.

Gage was sure that once the Turkish and Greek sides of their family received this videotaped session, they too, would be alarmed. It would take some serious planning to keep everyone up to speed, along with individualized plans to keep each of them safe. Although it seemed like an overwhelming task, there was no alternative if they were to be kept safe. And even that was no guarantee . . .

Tal tapped her fingers on the highly polished table. "We will approach this just like any other mission." She glanced to her right, looking at her fiancé, Wyatt Lockwood. "I'm putting a special team together, and we'll work out the bones of it. Then we'll put the muscle and finally, the skin on it. This is going to take a couple of weeks at least."

Robert gave his daughter an appreciative look as he leaned forward. "Until we can get a plan into place, we're all black ops. We know how to watch for potential threats, and we'll get through this and be the stronger for it."

After the family meeting, Gage felt Alexa

withdrawing again. It wasn't the same as it had been before the meeting; instead, she'd gone under the PTSD wave.

Since returning home a week ago, Alexa had succumbed to screaming nightmares every night, leaving both her and Gage sleepless and edgy. Gage, however, had additional concerns. Alexa had missed two appointments with her physician since returning home from Paris. She had muttered something about being "okay" and not needing another appointment, and Gage couldn't drag her to the doctor's office in nearby Alexandria, Virginia.

Dara, a pediatrics physician, had agreed to make a house call and come out to their farm and see how her fiancé's younger sister was doing. Gage was relieved; she had a low-key, maternal way about her, and her soft smile could bend steel. Alexa agreed to meet with her, and Gage was hopeful she could make some headway in getting the woman he loved so much to stop running and face her problems.

About an hour later, Dara arrived and stopped by Gage's office at their farmhouse. Normally, she was buoyant and smiling, but not today—not after getting the report about the threats from Sharan and Rasari. Gage asked her to come in. She was still the wearing cinnamon colored wool slacks, a blazer of the same color, and a white silk tee from her day at her clinic.

The colors set off her shoulder-length, straight blond hair.

"Alexa's in the office down at the end of the hall, first door on the left," he said, gesturing toward it. "Could you use some coffee?"

She rolled her eyes. "Right now, I think a stiff drink would be about right. But I'm pregnant now and alcohol is out of the question."

"Yeah, I think we all could go for one at this point," Gage agreed amiably.

"But coffee does sound wonderful."

"Great. I'm making a fresh pot. Can I bring you and Alexa some in her office? It'll be just a few minutes."

Dara reached out, hugging Gage. "Thanks, you're a doll." She released him and studied him, unable to hide her concern. "How are you holding up, Gage? You look really stressed out."

Gage walked to the kitchen to begin making the coffee as she followed him. "I'm okay," he lied.

Dara gave a ladylike snort, leaning against the granite counter near the sinks while he prepared their coffee. "Children lie better than you, Gage," she said, grinning.

He managed a faint smile. "Alexa isn't sleeping through the night. I thought it was bad before she left for Paris but now, she's had a screaming nightmare every night since her return."

"Hmm," she said, nodding. "Not unusual,

Gage. Has her doc ordered a mild sleep med for her?"

"She refuses to take medication."

"Well," Dara said, giving him an understanding look, "we'll see about that."

ALEXA MANAGED A warm, welcoming smile as Dara entered the room with two cups of coffee in her long, delicate hands. "Hey, how are you doing?" she asked Dara, standing up behind the desk and gratefully taking one of the coffee cups.

"Stressed out," she admitted, sitting down at her computer. "That board meeting was an eye opener. And being pregnant, my energy doesn't last as long, but I'm not complaining," Dara closed the door, taking the chair beside the desk where Alexa was on the computer.

Alexa glumly nodded. She loved Dara since having met her after Matt had rescued her from a near kidnapping in Afghanistan. The thirty-year-old physician was warm and a wonderful listener. Alexa was so happy that she and her brother, Matt, were going to get married next June in Kuşadası, Turkey, and then spend their honeymoon in cousin Angelo's mountain villa on the slopes of Mt. Olympus. Alexa was going to be one of her bridesmaids and was so looking forward to it. She fiercely loved her brother,

Matt. She wished only good things for this couple.

"You're looking really tired," Dara said, reaching out and touching Alexa's hand. "Are you having a tough time with nightmares from that capture by Rasari?"

Groaning, she muttered, "Yes. I swear, Dara, you're a mind reader sometimes."

"Not really. What I can do to help you?"

"I'd give anything to get a full night's sleep. Poor Gage, I'm waking him up with my screams, Dara. I told him I'd go out on the couch and sleep, but he refused to leave my side."

"Because he loves you, silly," Dara patted her hand. "He wants to help you and be there for you, Alexa."

"I know. If this was your problem, Dara, what would you do?"

Smiling a bit, Dara considered. "Well, since you've had two back-to-back horrific traumas, I think I'd want to change that energy."

"What do you mean?"

"When I was a resident physician, I worked sixteen or more hours a day—it was tough," Dara said. "And after a while, I felt numb, worn out, and behaved more like a robot than a human. Matt's already seen me in this mode, and when he sees it, he yanks me off to the Smoky Mountains where your parents have that wonderful cabin. And I can't tell you how much that revives me, puts me back together again and makes me feel whole. More important, I feel human again. No longer am I numb or robotic. My emotions are on tap again." She smiled softly. "Matt calls it a 'time out,' and I call it 'breaking the energy.'"

Giving Alexa a sympathetic look, Dara continued, "Is there somewhere you would love to go? Just to stay for a couple of months—with Gage, of course. You need to get away from here, Alexa. Just be free, be alone, be by yourself. To me, that helps more than anything else."

"Would it stop my nightmares?"

"Maybe not at first, but the more you're where you love to be, the more relaxed you'll feel. And as a doctor, I can predict that you'll get more sleep and have a lot fewer nightmares. How does that sound to you?"

"Better than taking sleep meds," Alexa grumped, sipping her coffee. Giving Dara a pleading look, she said, "I have to do something different, Dara. I've never admitted this to anyone, but I *do* feel like a robot. I'm numb inside. I feel dead . . ."

"That's how I feel when I get pushed beyond my emotional limits, too," Dara admitted. "If you were my patient, I'd Rx you to your favorite vacation spot for three months. You truly need downtime to heal, Alexa. No distractions, no working seven days a week, which is what I know you've been doing. You're hiding from your emotions, not working through them."

"I know," Alexa whispered. "I-I'm so scared of what I might do . . . I feel like a nuclear bomb ready to detonate."

"Right." Dara patted her forearm. "Listen, why don't you discuss this with Gage? There isn't a person alive who wants to help you more than he does. And he's the right man to have around. Besides, with what's going on, you need him as your personal security detail. He can keep watch over both of you until Tal, Wyatt, and Matt can get our family security plan in place."

"That makes good sense," Alexa admitted quietly, moving the cup slowly around between her hands. "And I wouldn't want to be alone, Dara. God, I get so scared. It just isn't like me at all, but honestly, I jump at my shadow sometimes."

"It won't hurt anything for you to take three months off, Alexa. You have Sarina, who's perfectly capable of filling in for you here at Artemis. And I think Dilara and Robert would love to see you get away for some downtime. What do you think?"

Alexa sensed a tiny glimmer of hope. It was the first time since Gage and the SEAL team had rescued her from that cave in Afghanistan.

"You're right, Dara. And I'm going down the hall to talk to Gage about it," she said with a hopeful smile. "I think he'll feel good about my vacation therapy too."

CHAPTER 5

G AGE WAS FIXING dinner when Dara came over and gave him a warm hug and kiss on the cheek.

"Hang in there," she told him. "Alexa and I had a good talk."

He smiled a little, his hands wet in the sink. "Do you know anything about snipers?" he asked her, taking a nearby towel off a hook to dry his hands.

"Well," she said tentatively, "just what Matt mentioned in passing. Why?"

He hung the towel back on the hook, holding her gaze. "Snipers have the patience of Job." Gage glanced down the hall toward the office where Alexa remained. "I'll never give up on her, Dara. I love her. You don't walk away from someone when the bad times hit. And right now, she's hurting a lot. I've got the love and patience to walk through it all, so don't worry, okay?" He squeezed her arm gently.

Dara gave him a look of relief. "Good. Because Gage, I think Alexa's ready to crash."

Nodding, he said, "Yeah, I think so too."

"I talked to her about getting away for three months, away from this job and its daily reminders of what she went through. No one can emotionally handle that all the time. I know how hard this is on the partner."

Gage shot her an understanding look. "You don't know about my past, Dara. I think if you did, you wouldn't be worried that I'd walk out and leave her when things got tough."

"Just know that I'm here for both of you," she said quietly. "Please, stay in touch with me, okay? You're a wonderful couple, and you deserve each other in the best of ways, Gage. I hate seeing both of you having to go through this crap."

"That makes three of us," he said wryly, seeing Dara's expression ease a bit. "Tell Matt hello from us, okay?"

"I will. Good night . . ."

GAGE STOPPED HIMSELF from going to Alexa, instead mulling over his brief chat with Dara. He hoped that talking with her had helped her understand that he was in for the long haul. As he busied himself cutting up green beans for the steamer, he heard the door quietly close down the hall. Normally, as a sniper, his heartbeat was slow and solid, whether he was targeting an HVT, high value target, or just relaxing here in their farmhouse.

But all those years of being a sniper out in the badlands of Afghanistan had given him heightened awareness of everything around him, whether or not there was a threat. In this case, his love for Alexa made him even more aware of potential danger.

"Hey," Alexa whispered, coming up and sliding her hands around his waist, resting her head against his back. "Mmm, smells good. What are you cooking for us tonight?"

"Hey, you," he grinned, turning and seeing the stress in her hazel eyes. "We have some leftover lamb, steamed green beans, and a salad. That sound good to you?"

Because Alexa had lost at least twenty pounds since being home, her appetite was usually nonexistent. Only when Gage had moved with her into the farmhouse, where he could cajole her into eating more, had she gained back at least six of those pounds. He felt her arms tighten around his torso.

"I'm not very hungry tonight, Gage . . ."

"We'll see," he murmured. Alexa wasn't

someone who could be pushed into anything. "How did your chat with Dara go?"

She sighed, moving her hands slowly up and down his shirtsleeves, needing his warmth, his solidity, and his soothing nature. Gage was the calm eye in the center of her hurricane of emotions, and she yearned to be with him whenever possible.

"It was interesting," she offered without going into detail.

"That sounds like a tease," he said, wishing he could do something to help Alexa sleep through the night. She couldn't go on like this much longer.

She smiled a little and nuzzled her cheek into his back, kissing the fabric across it. "I think she might have a good idea."

"Tell me about it," Gage offered, feeling her ambivalence, hearing it in her voice.

"Dara suggested I take time off from work and go someplace I'd like to stay for three months or so."

"Hmm, to decompress, right?" Gage finished cutting up the green beans, set the knife aside, and blotted his hands dry on the nearby towel. Gently, he eased her arms from around him so he could turn and pull Alexa against him. Just touching her sent him into a hunger to love her.

Alexa settled trustingly against him, looking up at him. "What do you think about it?" she asked cautiously.

He framed her face, looking deep into her troubled eyes and feeling her conflicting thoughts and desires. This wasn't the Alexa he knew from before, and it reinforced for him how shattered she'd been from her trauma in Afghanistan.

Grazing her lips with his, Gage asked, "More important, how does it feel to you, baby?"

She leaned heavily against him and searched his gaze, their noses nearly touching. "Honestly? I don't feel anything anymore, Gage . . ." She quickly amended herself. "I mean . . . when you love me . . . I do feel something. A lot, actually. I'm free of all that shit that's rolling around inside me, especially after I climax."

She rested her hands on his chest as he released her and allowed his hands to move lightly across her tense shoulders, massaging the tightness out of them.

"I have a story to tell you," Gage offered quietly.

"Okay," Alexa said, sensing this was important to him. She loved when he opened up to her about his past.

"After Jen was raped and murdered by that street gang and my father went after them and killed several of them—before they killed him . . ."

Alexa nodded. "Oh, Gage, I remember everything you told me about that awful day."

"After that, my mother went to pieces, and I was left all alone to deal with it. I can understand it far better right now than I did as a thirteen-year-old. I was in shock, just like she was, but my Dad had always told me I would be the man of the house if he didn't make it back from Iraq. I took his words seriously—but I never imagined he'd be killed on the streets of Chicago." Gage lifted his fingers, moving them through her silky strands, watching her eyes grow less shadowed. His touch always brought Alexa back to her core center.

"But what did all that do to you, Gage? When you first told me what happened, I couldn't imagine how you felt. But now, after what's happened to me, I think I can deeply understand a little of what you went through."

He cupped her hips gently against his. Their intimacy and the trust they shared always overwhelmed and humbled him. "I'm sure you do. Others can't understand, even though they may want to try. But if someone hasn't gone through a similar trauma, he or she can't imagine what it does to you inside and out. So when you were talking about not feeling anything . . ."

"Yes?"

"Well, I understand. I was completely numb emotionally after Jen and Dad were murdered. I felt like you: hollowed out, like an untethered ball rolling around in the sky. I couldn't cry. I couldn't feel anything, Alexa. That went on for months."

"You had to devote your attention to your mother, Gage. You were never given a chance to work through your own grief, were you?"

He gave her a sad smile. "No, I had no one. But you do," he said, rocking her a little in his arms. "And now you have an opportunity to unplug from the past. I feel strongly you should take it, Alexa. I never got such an offer, and looking back, it took me five years to start feeling again. I didn't cry until my mom died when I was twenty-three and in the Marine Corps. I was on duty and couldn't be there for her, and it shattered me. And for the first time, I cried for all my lost family. I never cried so hard, so long, in all my life. And for two years afterward, I'd suddenly cry for no reason at all." Grimacing, he added hoarsely, "It was grief, old grief, making its way up and out of me, I suppose."

"But you had no one to hold you or help you," Alexa whispered, searching his dark, turbulent gaze.

Shrugging, he said, "No, I didn't. But that's just how it goes, baby." He grazed her cheek. "In your case though, you have me, you have your family, and you have many, many friends who support and love you."

"I can't even imagine getting through what you did alone, Gage. You're so much stronger than I am!"

"Well," he said wryly, "there's an old saying that God doesn't give you any more than you can bear. That was one of my mom's favorite sayings, and I grew up with that philosophy. So when my family was suddenly taken away from me, I figured God had given me the strength to get through it, and I put myself in charge of doing exactly that."

Alexa gnawed on her lower lip, looking away for a moment. Smoothing her fingertips across his chest, she asked, "Do you think that my staying at my post here at Artemis is like digging into an open wound? That it's not allowing me to heal—that it's reopened because I'm reminded of it daily?"

"I love how self-aware you are, Alexa," Gage said gruffly, giving her a spontaneous hug. "Yes, I do think it's working against you. I talked to Becka about this very topic weeks ago and she said the same thing. You jumped from the frying pan into the fire, baby. You came out of that sexual assault and kidnapping in Afghanistan, turned in your officer's commission, and then marched right into Artemis and took over that position."

He sighed and gave her a tender look. "You read visceral reports from the field, from other Delos charities, and they were about child abuse, rape, and sexual assault. It had to trigger you, trigger memories of what you went through."

He skimmed her hair, kissing her wrinkled brow. "I know how much you love helping people. It's such a part of your core essence, who you are. You're a dead ringer for your mom, Dilara. She's built the same way emotionally as you are. And all she knows how to do is to serve those who have less. It's an admirable gene and trait, but in your case, Alexa, it's not allowing you to heal up properly. Becka, Dara, and your whole family feel strongly that you should take three months away from your job here. Sarina can take over for you for that timeframe. It will be in good hands."

Alexa rested her head against his brow, her heart filled with love for this man of hers. Gage had gone through so much—he'd lost his entire family. She hadn't lost hers.

"A part of me has been destroyed," she whispered, closing her eyes, feeling his hands move up her back and cup her shoulders.

"Yes," he huskily admitted, holding her tightly. "It's sort of like losing a limb. But it doesn't mean you can't live with what you've got left, baby."

"Like you do?"

He snorted softly and nodded. "Yeah, like I do."

"I guess I'm really lucky and I don't even realize it."

"Oh, don't go there," Gage said with a coaxing smile. "Trauma affects every person differently. A car crash might make a person swear never to drive again. Another person will get over it and move on. Trauma is individualized, Alexa. No one can ever judge how it has affected you, how it has changed you, or how much you'll heal up from it."

"Becka said the same thing."

"Becka is right. Most of us have to hear the same thing several times before we'll change or learn from other people's experiences or knowledge."

"I hear you," she admitted. "I guess there's a part of me that's very proud, and I'm afraid my family will think less of me. I worry Tal will see me as weak, or a failure . . ."

"Oh, baby," he crooned, holding her tightly against him. "No one sees you in that light. They understand. Tal is concerned about you, just as we all are. But she sure doesn't see you as a failure." He kissed her hair. "In fact, Tal and I were both thinking of asking you to take some healing time."

"Tal really knows people well," Alexa agreed quietly.

"Look," Gage said, "we all hit brick walls, Alexa. I hit a lot them at an early age. Tal hit her brick wall just recently, and is still just recovering when she almost bled out on that ridge in the mountains of Afghanistan. Every person on this earth hits hard walls and gets knocked down sooner or later."

Lips quivering, Alexa said, "I guess it's my turn."

"We all get a turn, believe me," he said, releasing her. "And now, it's our turn to eat. Will you be ready in about thirty minutes?"

Stepping away, Alexa said, "Sure. And I want to talk to Tal after dinner and see if she's okay with me taking a hiatus for a while."

"Will you talk with your parents, too?" he asked.

"Absolutely. My dad believes that many heads are better than one when making a major decision."

He smiled, pulling the plates down from the cabinet to put on the table. "And he's a general." The joke wasn't lost on either of them. So much of the tension she'd carried in her face was gone. Alexa was easily moved one way or another, moment to moment. He wished he understood more about astrology. Were moon in Pisces people like that? Like thermometers in their surroundings? She had told him in that big warehouse in Bagram as they sorted out the charity clothing and shoes about her astrology signs. He found it curious that she used astrology at all, but darned if she hadn't convinced him that there was something to it.

Laughing softly, Alexa said, "That he is, but to us, he's Dad in Chief. He taught us how to work with people, how to draw them out to find out what they're really thinking and feeling. He's very astute at getting people to open up about their thoughts and ideas."

"He's a rare bird, pardon the pun, among the Air Force officers, then," Gage said, teasing her.

"My dad is an incredible man." She leaned over, kissing Gage's cheek. "Like you . . ."

TWO DAYS LATER, Alexa was in the farmhouse by herself. Gage had stayed late at Artemis because a mission had suddenly popped up and it required him, Tal, Wyatt, and Matt to remain there to resolve the issue. She had come home early, around two p.m., the October sun shining and warming up the afternoon. It was her turn to cook dinner tonight, and she'd gotten out a roasting chicken and placed it on the kitchen counter. Looking out the L-shaped windows covered with ruffled white curtains, she felt a rush of pleasure as orange and gold leaves fluttered down to the ground from the red maple near their white rail fence.

Her mind was on the meeting earlier in the day, about the steps the family would take to avoid one of them being kidnapped, as she had been. Gage had suggested that, in their case, they get a dog. The dog needn't be a combat assault type, like a Belgian Malinois, but perhaps a Lab or retriever that would excel as a watchdog.

Alexa liked the idea. The farmhouse felt empty without a dog. She'd grown up in her family with two black Labs as friends, babysitters, and guards for herself and her siblings. Gage had teased her that she needed something to nurture, give her own brand of mothering to, and she smiled faintly as she set the table for them. Alexa knew he was right: she had to "mother" something, and getting a puppy seemed like a great idea to her. That way, like today, she wouldn't feel so vulnerable in the house by herself. Before her trauma in Afghanistan, things like this would never bother her. Now, being alone made her tense and wary. There *was* a threat, and alone in this house, she felt unprotected. It was a helluva fall from being a confident, brazen combat pilot in Afghanistan to her newly precarious position. Alexa didn't like feeling weak or unsafe.

Only Gage made her feel safe, completely safe, and that was erroneous, too. He was human, and as much as he loved her and wanted to guard her, to give her that sense of protection, he couldn't be with her 24/7. And right now he was fifteen miles away at a mission planning meeting.

Becka had told her that cortisol was the culprit, making her constantly feel raw and on edge.

Her body was pouring cortisol continuously into her bloodstream, unchecked. It wasn't always a bad hormone, but when a person's life was threatened, it gave the individual heightened alertness, awareness, and an almost psychic sense of where an enemy was located so the person could avoid the threat and live another day. Cortisol worked hand-in-hand with adrenaline, which caused the "fight-or-flight" response when a person was under threat.

Frowning, she pulled out veggies from the refrigerator to make Gage and herself a salad for dinner. Just as she turned, she caught a flash of something dark out of the corner of her eye. Instantly, Alexa gasped, her heart going into a wild, pounding action. She dropped the vegetables. What had she seen?

Whatever it was, it was outside. She felt terror racing through her and stood immobilized, trying to think.

Was it someone sent by Rasari to recapture her? Her mind went wild and frantic, the urge to run nearly overwhelming. At the same time, Alexa was paralyzed by the unexpected situation, her heart pounding so loud she couldn't hear anything else in her ears.

Hyper-alert, every sense blown wide open, she looked toward the front door, taking everything in from every possible angle. Her skin was chilled, her hearing heightened. Who had she glimpsed?

Alexa waited, hoping someone would knock at the front door. Had she locked the door? God, no, she hadn't! Oh, why hadn't she? What was she thinking? If it was a hit man from Rasari, all he had to do was twist the doorknob, waltz in, and recapture her.

Gun! Where was a gun?

Gage had a locked gun cabinet, but it was in their bedroom, behind the sliding doors of their clothing closet. Her mind calculated how long it would take her to get from the kitchen to the bedroom. Feeling helpless, her gaze riveted on the front door, Alexa tried to think.

She'd flown an A-10 combat jet and had never choked up like she was doing right now. She'd thought coolly and calmly through the fog of war to pickle her bombs on a target, or to swoop down out of the sky, using the .50 caliber Gatling gun in the nose of her fighter, to push back the enemy in Afghanistan.

She had never hesitated. Everything she did in her heavily armored cockpit was from thousands of hours of training that translated into smooth-functioning muscle memory.

Now, muscle memory was no longer within her. She wasn't in the safety of the cockpit of her A-10. She was vulnerable, with no pistol on her, no weapon to defend herself with, should a man come through that unlocked door to capture her.

A man who would take her away to Rasari to become a sex slave.

Revulsion twisted through Alexa, her breathing ragged and choppy. Why couldn't she move? Frustration and terror wound through her.

She gasped, seeing a tall man in jeans and a white shirt walk past the window once again. Blinking, Alexa saw a patch on the black jacket he wore. It was a man from the local electric company! Only then did her cortisol charged brain realize he had his company truck parked in the gravel lot in front of their farmhouse. The man had read the electric meter and was returning to his truck to move on to the next house.

Oh, God! Alexa bent over, her hands on her knees, gasping for air, trying to separate her body from her dazed mind. She was shaking, chilled, and scared. As the adrenaline left her bloodstream, she felt weakness overcome her. She stumbled to the couch in the living room and sat down, her head between her hands, trying to slow her choppy breathing.

Humiliation blazed through her. The combat pilot she'd been and the weepy, helpless woman she was now were two different people. Would she ever return to her previous confident self? Her mind bounced around for another hour as every noise, every creak, even leaves slapping against the kitchen window seemed like mini-alarms.

If only Gage were home. She could talk to him about everything . . . anything. What would he think of her overreaction to the utility man going to read the electric meter?

Her brain saw everything as a potential threat. *Everything!*

Finally, Alexa forced herself to stand upright, her knees still feeling wonky. She straightened, mouth tight, forcing herself to focus through the cortisol ravaging her inwardly. Somewhere, somehow, she had to fight back, fight the hormone and get on with her life. She bent down, picking up the head of lettuce, the bag of carrots, celery, and a lone onion. There had to be something in the world besides medication that would stop the leaking of cortisol into her bloodstream twenty-four hours a day.

Placing the veggies on the counter, she saw Gage pulling into the driveway in their silver Kia SUV. Relief surged through her. Gage was home! He was here. He loved her. He protected her when she felt so raw and without a skin to protect herself.

Would he tire of taking care of her? He'd fallen in love with the confident A-10 combat pilot, not this fainthearted wimp who couldn't defend herself. Wouldn't Gage grow weary of always taking care of her? In her imagination, she saw him walking away from her, unable to deal with her violent emotional ups and downs. And if he did, she knew she couldn't go on. She had nothing left inside to help her climb this mountain—one that seemed absolutely impossible for her to scale alone.

CHAPTER 6

G AGE NOTICED HOW pale Alexa was when he entered their home. She was busy in the kitchen making a salad for their dinner.

"Hey," he called, "we got done a little early on that unexpected mission."

Alexa lifted her head and smiled a little as Gage closed the front door, locked it, and then turned, sauntering into the cozy, L-shaped kitchen. "Good. Did it turn out all right?"

Gage nodded. "Yeah, tempest in a teapot. Wyatt's handling the rest of it."

"It will be an hour before we eat. Is that okay?"

Gage came over, noticing a slight trembling in her hands as she cut into the head of lettuce. He leaned over, kissing her cheek. "Everything all right, baby?"

Alexa felt herself break inside. She put the

knife aside as he slid his arm around her waist, standing there like the bulwark he'd always been to her. "I can't fool you, can I?" she said, giving him an apologetic look.

"When you love someone, you become attuned to them," Gage said simply, kissing her temple. "What happened?" There was turmoil in her eyes, and Gage, trained to be sensitive as a sniper, knew that Alexa often kept secrets from him. He knew she worried that he'd get tired of her behavior and one-day walk away.

He snorted—as if! Getting a firsthand look at PTSD and the pervasive damage cortisol did to someone only made him more committed to Alexa. There were times, though, when he wondered if she really believed that he was there for the long haul.

Wiping her hands on a towel, she moved out of his loose embrace, pulling a bright yellow ceramic bowl over for the chopped veggies. In as few words as possible, she told Gage what had happened earlier that day, watching for any signs of disappointment in him.

Gage leaned against the counter, his arms across his chest as she shared what had happened when the utility man had come to read the farmhouse's electric meter. His mouth tightened as she finished. She was worried that she'd overreacted to the strange man who had suddenly popped up out of nowhere.

"Did you see him drive in?" Gage asked.

Shaking her head, Alexa whispered, "No. I should have looked, but I focused on that jacket I saw come past the window and I just . . . well . . . I overreacted as usual, Gage."

He nodded and walked over to her after she'd put the bowl of salad into the fridge. "Come here," he said, pulling her into his arms. She crumpled against him and allowed him to support her. She slid her arms around his waist, clinging to him like a frightened child.

"You did the best you could. Your brain probably thought it was Rasari or one of his men coming to get you." She nodded, her embrace tightening as he guessed the truth. Alexa had left that out of her explanation, and Gage knew she was humiliated by her overreaction, but she couldn't help it.

"I . . ." Alexa stumbled, her voice strained, her cheek pressed against his chest. "I . . . panicked. I thought he was a hit man from Rasari either coming to kill me or kidnap me again." Alexa loathed feeling vulnerable 24/7. When would this end?

Gage embraced her a little tighter.

"And then I realized I hadn't locked the front door, Gage. How stupid is that? My imagination blew up after that, and I was standing here in the kitchen, literally frozen in place. I couldn't move. I knew the gun was in the locked cabinet in our bedroom closet, and that I should run across the living room and get to it, get a pistol out to protect myself. But I couldn't think straight! I knew in some part of my brain what to do, but I was frozen. It was awful." She pressed her face deep into the folds of his shirt.

"Did you know that when a fawn is lying in a field, hidden, and a predator comes by, the fawn freezes?" Gage asked, kissing the shell of her ear. "Freezing is one way that your mind works to save you."

"I-I didn't think of that."

"It's a survival mechanism," he said quietly, easing Alexa away from him just enough to meet her confused gaze. "Your brain selected freezing instead of running for the gun cabinet. That's all."

"I couldn't move, Gage. I felt trapped. I felt like that hit man was coming through the door and he'd see me." Her voice became hoarse. "I-I thought he'd just grab me, put me in flex cuffs, and haul me out of here. I couldn't stop my mind from thinking those things. I just couldn't . . ."

"It's all right to feel that way, baby . . ."

Just Gage's low, calming voice helped Alexa stabilize, and she saw the patience in his shadowed face, felt his confidence in her, helping her to ramp down from her out of control feelings. "I hated myself, Gage. I hated that I was so scared I couldn't move. I've been a damned combat pilot! I never froze on the job, ever!"

Gage nodded. "When we get fractured, we aren't who we used to be. I know from the time I lost my sister and dad. I changed, too."

"Did you ever get back to the real you?" she asked, her voice a ragged whisper.

How badly Gage wanted to tell her that everything would be all right. But it wouldn't be. There was such hopelessness in Alexa's widened eyes that he tried his best to reassure her.

"Every time we have a life event, it changes us," he told her, holding her stricken gaze. "But it doesn't mean we're weaker. Sometimes we just have to break in order to become stronger. I know it seems illogical, but it's what I've found for myself, Alexa. It took me years to paste myself back together again. It was painful, and it was slow. In time, I saw a pattern in my healing process. I'd have good days, and then I'd cycle down and have two or three bad days, where I questioned my sanity and wondered if I'd ever get better. Then the good days would come back and give me hope, and I'd see a glimmer down at the end of that long, dark tunnel."

"Didn't you get tired of all that cycling up and down?"

He smiled a little, his fingers grazing her hair. "Sure. All the time."

"How did you get through it?"

"I concentrated on helping my mom. She

was my focus. I just put everything I was feeling on the back burner."

"My therapist, Becka, doesn't want me to do that."

"Well, our cases are different, Alexa. I was in shock. You're experiencing PTSD. Now shock, as I understand it, can be like a mild case of PTSD, but eventually, most people work out of it. The older I got, the less cycling I experienced. My focus and concentration, although impaired, was not affected as yours is right now."

"Becka says it will get better with time," Alexa said wearily. "I just can't concentrate like I used to."

"That's the cortisol effect," Gage informed her. He saw fewer shadows and less terror in her eyes. Alexa was one of those people who could be talked down when the cycle was right, and at those times she responded readily. Gage was convinced that this ability would help Alexa heal faster than he had. And he hadn't had anyone to talk him down.

Alexa clung to him, needing him desperately, and eagerly surrendered as he lowered his mouth to hers. She opened her lips, offering to give all that was within her while taking his love and the hope he offered her every single day. She relaxed as he did this again, absorbing her love, her pain, her trauma, and dissolving it with his tongue, his probing lips.

She was immediately lost in the delicious heat of his mouth caressing hers. She enjoyed kissing Gage as much as he enjoyed kissing her. Gage was always attractive to her, even during her down days. Now, as she was pulling out of them, she was hungry for his male scent, his taste, the moistness of his breath as he claimed her mouth. It was such a relief when Gage made the world go away, feeding her hopes for a better one. He pasted together the fragments of her fractured self, offering her the love that would help her heal those chasm-wide cracks within herself.

Easing away from her wet, soft lips, Gage murmured, "Let me help you get dinner on the table. I have some ideas I want to talk to you about later."

"Of course," she whispered, still caught up in the promise of his kiss.

He smiled a little and led her over to the table, pulling out her chair. "Have a seat, and let's talk while I put the food on the table for us."

Alexa gave him a wry look. "This is your fault, Hunter. You kissed me and threw me into another world, a wonderful one. And I don't want to come back." She watched him preen beneath her softly spoken compliment. Alexa knew she needed to tell Gage more often how much she loved him, how grateful she was for his care. This man possessed such humility that he was quiet about his accomplishments, which were many. He always gave others the credit instead of himself.

"I'll gladly take the fall on that one," he said with a grin. Soon enough, Gage had brought the chicken and salad to their kitchen table. As he sat down at her elbow, he said, "Becka, Tal, and I were wondering where your favorite place for a three-month vacation might be." He placed half of a baked breast onto her plate, knowing that if she did it herself, it would be a tiny amount, and he wanted her to eat more than that. Using a ladle, he poured over a fragrant white gravy on the poultry.

"I know we talked a little bit about this after Dara left, but I was too upset still to give you some ideas. I love the Florida Keys," she said. "I love the ocean, the warm waters to swim, snorkel, and scuba dive in. They have beautiful undersea coral there. Have you ever been there?"

"Not to Florida," Gage said, spooning the salad on her plate. "I've been to the Pacific Ocean, and I went through boot camp at Parris Island in South Carolina, and swam in the Harbor River that empties into Atlantic Ocean while there. But I never set foot in the Atlantic itself."

"My family has a winter home in Key Largo, Florida. It's a beautiful two-story white house on Island Drive. The John Pennekamp Coral Reef State Park is about five miles from our house. As kids growing up, we kayaked, snorkeled, found lots of shells, and had tons of adventures just playing along the shore."

"Sounds nice," Gage said. He noticed Alexa was eating a little bit more. Maybe he could get her to regain her lost weight when they took the three-month sabbatical.

She met his gaze. "Could you come with me? Can Tal really afford to have you gone for three months, Gage? Or maybe you can fly in to see me some weekends," she said hopefully.

Gage heard the concern in her low voice. "We're on the same wavelength. I talked to Tal about that this afternoon," he said, sopping up the white gravy with a piece of bread. "She says I can't be out of touch because Artemis is ramping up hiring in all departments. But," he continued, giving her a hopeful look, "to resolve that issue, she's having Human Resources go through the resumes of current snipers looking for a job with us. Tal is asking Wyatt to take care of the daily work while I'm gone. But the resumes of snipers will be sent directly to me for consideration. One of them will be hired and act as a liaison for Mission Planning in my absence. But if things get dicey, Wyatt can always Skype me and I'll work with him from Key Largo, when necessary. That means if you want my mangy hide along for those three months, you can have me. How do you feel about that?" He gazed into her widening eyes, seeing hope bring them to life again.

Gage would never have insisted upon going if Alexa didn't invite him. He knew that sometimes people wanted to be alone, but Gage felt she needed company right now. There would be other times when she might want alone time—later, when she was stronger. Right now, she was devastated by her kidnapping by Rasari. The predatory monster was never caught, nor were the men with him. So it ended in a cold trail, much to everyone's unhappiness. He was now safely in Malgar where he could not be touched by first-world countries that wanted him. It just compounded Alexa's initial wound, deepening it, tearing up what healing she'd already begun.

"I want you with me." She reached out, gripping his large, callused hand.

He managed a relieved grin as he curved his fingers around hers. "Yeah, I want to be with you too, if it feels right, Alexa."

Her cheeks flushed pink, sudden light coming to her hazel eyes, hope and a flicker of humor in them.

"But I don't know how to kayak or snorkel. Maybe you can teach me—if you're up to it," he teased.

"Oh, I'd love to!" she grinned, suddenly feeling a ton of weight sloughing off her shoulders. "You'll pick it up so easily, Gage, so don't worry about that."

"Well, what *should* I worry about? Those nasty gators down in the Keys?"

"Hey," Alexa gave him a broad smile. "No worries. We'll be in Coral State Park, and the rangers there know where the big ones live. They know their movements, and the gators are most active at dawn and dusk. You and I would be in the water during the day, not at night, so I wouldn't be too concerned about it."

"Well, just between us, I'm going to strap a Ka-Bar knife on my lower leg whenever we go into the water."

She chortled, giddy with excitement. "That's my man! Ever the guardian."

"Yep," he declared, delighted that Alexa was so enthusiastic about the idea. Gage loved his woman, and he wanted nothing more than to see those golden lights back in her eyes, just as they were right now. Everyone who loved her had begged Alexa to take a sabbatical, and he was sure their support had helped her make the decision.

"I'm going to fly us down there in my Stearman biplane," she said, releasing his hand. "I need to get to Andy, my mechanic, over at the airport to make sure he's got the inspections up to date before we take off."

Chuckling, Gage saw her dive into her food as if not even realizing she was eating. Alexa was now eating with gusto. He actually wished he'd put more on her plate in the first place. "Do you snorkel for fish, spear them, and bring them back to eat?" he wondered.

"We can't do it in the park, but there are bays nearby that are available. My dad is usually the chief spear fisher, and I'm rusty, but maybe we can learn together. I love fresh fish. There are lobsters around, too. And we can buy shrimp at a local fish market."

"I was pretty much raised on meat and potatoes," Gage admitted. "But I'm willing to stretch my taste boundaries."

Aglow, Alexa said, "This will be so wonderful! I feel so much better, Gage."

"Good," he murmured, hopeful that this vacation would help relieve Alexa's symptoms. "I think this will be good for both of us. Things have been hectic since we met in Afghanistan, and three months of downtime could be just the right remedy for both of us."

After dinner, Alexa asked Gage to sit with her at her Mac computer's big screen in their home office. She brought up a map of Key Largo and then pulled up some photos she'd taken several years earlier of her parents' two-story white home with green shutters. Gage sat next to her, their thighs touching as she deftly brought up photos of the nearby state park. Excitement surged through her as she described what they were seeing, and he savored this special time with her.

She turned and gave him a wicked look. "By the way, have you ever made love in the ocean?"

"No," he said. "I never really thought of it."

"It's like when we use our huge shower, Gage. The ocean is deliciously warm, clear, and beautiful. I know a nice little spot near a mangrove area that's perfect for it."

"Sounds good to me," he agreed, his eyes sparkling.

She chuckled. "You perk up every time sex is mentioned, Hunter. Why am I not surprised?"

He laughed with her and rubbed her shoulders. They felt remarkably pliable, with no tension in them. Just maybe these three months would help release Alexa from the prison of her fears.

Gage was hooking into her excitement about going to the Keys for her sabbatical. "You know, I don't think about sex as 'sex' when it comes to you," he confided. "I 'make love' with you, baby." He saw the flush in her cheeks deepen, and the look of yearning in her eyes told him she had, for now, come back to him.

"Thank you for that," Alexa whispered, touching his rugged, unshaved face. "I've never been as well loved as I have by you, Gage . . ."

He felt an erection stir. It always happened when Alexa used that smoky voice of hers after she became aroused. *Tonight could be the night*, he thought. Such times might happen once a week since her PTSD had taken over their lives. Her therapist had warned them that sexual needs were often suppressed in the process, and she'd been right, but Gage didn't love Alexa because they had sex together. It was only one of the delicious gifts that came with loving her.

He looked at his watch. It was ten p.m. "Want to go to the shower and show me how to swim with the fishes?"

Her response was immediate, her eyes narrowing, her lips parting. He could hardly wait to release his swelling erection from his jean's imprisoning zipper.

"I think I'm ready for a nice, long shower with you, Hunter." Her voice was low and husky.

Gage didn't waste a minute. He stood and pulled his chair away from hers. "Come on, baby, we deserve this . . ."

MOONLIGHT WAS PEEKING through the dark blue winter drapes in their bedroom. Gage settled Alexa's damp, warm body against his. She made a low purring sound, snuggling against him, her head resting on his shoulder, her arm thrown across his torso. He liked that she slid one long leg around his, getting as close to him as possible.

"Comfy?" he growled against her hair, holding her tightly against him, inhaling the fragrance of her favorite rose scented soap.

"Mmm, I'm more than comfy. You give me the best orgasms, Gage. I don't know how you do it . . ." she grinned.

He threaded his fingers through her damp hair. "Well, you definitely returned the favor, Ms. Culver. You had your game on back there in the shower."

He felt her shake with silent laughter. Alexa was so loving when she let herself be fully vulnerable with Gage. In fact, since meeting her, her love was helping him to truly open up to a woman in ways he'd never known. And, more than ever, Gage was coming to appreciate their time together after making love. That was when the most important issues came up for them to explore.

"Gage?" she asked him tentatively.

"Hmm?"

"I . . . I really want to be to carry your baby," she said quietly, then waited for his response.

He held her close, feeling her heart against his ribs and the pillowy softness of her breasts. Frowning, he tried to choose his words carefully. "What about your PTSD symptoms?"

"I know," she sighed sadly. "I talked to Dara about it. I asked if the cortisol symptoms would go away if I were with child, and she said no, they wouldn't."

"So you'd still have the up and down cycles?"

"Yes. And Dara said that when a woman is pregnant, she's already got a lot of things going on hormonally. Everything is accentuated, especially the emotions. That would be multiplied with the influence of the cortisol when PTSD symptoms arose. I'd be even more sensitive. I would cry more easily . . . things like that . . ."

"That would be pretty difficult, wouldn't it, given your PTSD?" he said softly.

"Yes. And we're talking physical sensitivity, too. I can't control the cortisol. Becka explained that the hormone is like a faucet you can't turn off."

"Baby, I worry about you," Gage turned on his side and intently studied her shadowed face. He saw the hope in her eyes and didn't want to bring her down. "I know how important it is for us to start a family. Why don't we take this three-month sabbatical and see how you respond to it?"

"That sounds like a good idea." She closed her eyes and whispered, "I'm so damned wishy-washy emotionally, Gage. It drives me nuts."

A wry smile tugged at one corner of his mouth as he leaned over, pressing a light kiss on her pouting lips. "You've always wanted to carry babies," he pointed out. "And you're going to be an incredible mother, just like your own. Dilara raised you kids right, and you'll do the same for the new generation coming into the family."

Gage had a burning desire to create a baby. He yearned for a family of his own again. Nothing was more important to him. His whole life had been interrupted when he was thirteen, and he'd never told anyone, except Alexa, how he longed to have children around, to be a father, as his heroic father had been to him and Jen. He silently prayed that he and Alexa could create a beautiful little girl.

More than anything, Gage would like to call her Jen, after his sister, whom he still loved so much that some days he could hardly bear the grief over her loss. If they had a daughter, he felt it would help him finally heal from that open wound.

Closing her eyes, Alexa tipped her chin up to meet Gage's warm, loving mouth. She hummed, arching her back, pressing her breasts wantonly against him. She felt his cock, which rested between them, hardening and thickening. Sure, they'd already made love in the shower, but just talking about becoming a mother to his children, made Alexa's whole lower body ignite with the possibility.

"Gage . . . what if . . . what if I went off the Pill while we're in the Keys?" She opened her eyes, looking deep into his blue ones. "Would that bother you?"

Pressing himself against her soft, rounded belly, he groaned as she allowed her hand to languish around his cock, stroking it lightly, setting him on fire. This woman could turn him on in a heartbeat! Her strong fingers massaged his erection and he felt his balls tighten, pulling against his body.

"Let's talk about this tomorrow morning," he groaned. He knew that he was going to love Alexa right now, and he found her more than ready as she allowed his hand to cup her ass, his fingers trailing down that curved crevice to encounter her damp, wet curls below. He breathed in her musky scent and found himself spinning out of control, feeling as if he were losing his ability to think.

It was like being hurled into a cauldron of raw animal hunger—and this wasn't the first time. There was an ancient part deep within him that wanted to take her hard and fast, mate with her so she would conceive. No more words, just action, making their mutual dream come true.

Alexa quivered, giving a little cry as he lightly stroked her entrance with his fingers, easing into her, feeling her violently react in the best of ways to his slow, teasing intrusion. He liked feeling that quiver rippling through her. It told him she was hot and eager. He loved those days, like up on the crown of that hill when they'd gone hiking, when he felt like a caveman as he made love to his woman.

All he knew was that her sexy fragrance triggered an ancient inborn part of himself, the animal that lurked in the background, that charged ferociously through him when he slid his hard cock into her beautiful, tight, wet channel.

She was so natural and loving. Despite going through the PTSD with her, Gage no longer worried about their personal sex life. At first, he'd been concerned that Alexa would consider him just another man, like those who had assaulted and injured her. Becka had been worried about it, too. But somehow their love had remained pure and fostered a healthy connection between them, no matter what else was happening.

Rolling over, covering her, his cock resting against her belly, Gage took her hands and eased them above her head. Alexa gave him a languorous look, raising her hips, inviting him inside.

"You know, you're a very dangerous woman," Gage muttered, running his hand down to her breasts, teasing a hardened nipple. Her eyes closed, her lips parted, and her breathing grew ragged as he continued to run his thumb back and forth over the hard nub. She couldn't lie still beneath him, hips twisting, wanting him, little pleading noises filling her throat, begging him to enter her.

And he was ready. Oh, so ready! Gage liked foreplay time like this. All they had to do was enjoy one another on a purely physical level. Alexa had climaxed twice in the shower, and he knew she had another climax or two yet to come.

He slid one hand down her flank and then released her wrists, kneeling between her opened thighs, running his hands lightly up and down them, listening to her beg him to please her with whimpers, to move inside her.

Finally, he'd found a woman who held nothing back. It was heart-to-heart, body-to-body, with their souls melting into one another just as they were doing right now.

CHAPTER 7

D ARA MCKINLEY STOOD up and walked around her clinic desk when Alexa Culver entered. "So nice to see you!" she said, hugging Alexa. "When I looked at the schedule this morning, I saw your name." She released her. "Is everything okay, Alexa?"

"I needed to talk to you professionally," Alexa admitted, sitting down in a bright red chair in front of Dara's large desk. Dara wore a white lab coat, her stethoscope around her neck, her blond hair caught up with two gold barrettes that Alexa recognized. Dilara Culver must have gifted Dara with them. Alexa saw the delicate hammered Turkish designs on the long barrettes.

"Okay," Dara said, sitting down. She pulled over Alexa's file, opening it as she started up her computer. "What's going on?"

Alexa glanced out the window of the clinic,

just a few blocks away from the hospital where Dara had been a resident. Now, Dara had privileges at the medical facility. The early November sky was murky, threatening rain or snow. Alexa turned her attention to the pediatrician. "Gage has been doing a lot of online research about my high cortisol."

"That makes sense. What's he found?" Dara asked, curious.

Alexa pulled printed copies of papers from her briefcase and slid them across the desk to Dara. "Are you familiar with a new branch of medicine known as functional medicine?"

Dara took the papers, quickly perusing them. "Yes, I've heard of it. But honestly, I don't know a whole lot about it," she smiled. "Why don't you tell me what's important about it and how it might affect your high cortisol?"

"I liked their motto," Alexa said. "'Changing the way we do medicine, and the medicine we do.' Apparently they work with nutrition, alternative medicine, and lifestyle choices, which all play into a person's ailment."

Dara studied the copies she had in hand. "Well, I don't see anything here that could be harmful to you. I'm in agreement that a patient's history, their environment, and the meds they take and other influences should all be taken into account before looking at an overall plan to help the patient with his or her issue or disease."

"And a lot of doctors don't do that," Alexa said. "I know you do. I think you're a functional medicine specialist doc by instinct." Alexa smiled a little.

"Could be." Dara placed the printed out sheets to one side. "I'll take these home with me tonight, Alexa, and really get into their medical philosophy. But where do you see this type of doctor helping you with your high cortisol?"

"Well, let me back up. When Gage found this material, I got really excited, Dara. It gave me hope. There's a directory of physicians who are functional medicine specialists, and there is a PA, a physician's assistant, named Taylor Douglas who has a clinic in Wind River, Wyoming. Her focus is dealing with high cortisol and PTSD symptoms!"

"Really?" Dara sat up, and Alexa handed her another sheet of paper.

"Yes. She gives each patient a saliva test and then sends the results to a lab to be checked. On her website, she shows some of her patients' before-and-after results three months after giving them an 'adaptogen.' That's a compound created by a certain company to shut off out-of-control cortisol so that the pituitary gland can start to control it instead, as it should. If the cortisol is shut down, then a lot of the PTSD symptoms stop immediately. And according to Taylor Douglas's literature, they remain stopped unless there is another huge trauma in the person's life. And even if there is, they can take the adaptogen under a medical practitioner's guidance and stop the cortisol from constantly pouring into the bloodstream. In other words, the adaptogen acts like a shut-off valve for a faucet that is pouring out water. It shuts off the cortisol and the PTSD symptoms go away forever."

Her voice rose in excitement as she pulled a number of other papers from her briefcase and spread them out across Dara's desk. "Look at these results," she said, showing Dara a chart. "They're all from ex-military men and women who have gone to Ms. Douglas for their PTSD symptoms. They took the saliva test, got the results back, and you can see they all have higher than normal cortisol levels."

She traced the chart with her fingertip and Dara frowned, studying it intently.

"Then," Alexa went on eagerly, "Ms. Douglas gave them an adaptogen for thirty days, and most of the people reported that their anxiety disappeared in two to four days!"

Alexa's voice rose as she pointed to the "after" graph. "Three months after that initial round of the adaptogen, the subjects retook the saliva test. Look at this, Dara. This is amazing!"

She pointed to the second set of lab test results. "All of their cortisol is now within or near normal limits, and they all reported that the horrible anxiety I live with was gone, and it hadn't returned. Taylor has followed these vets, and their cortisol levels remain normal." She looked up at Dara. "Can you believe that a single thirty-day course of taking this adaptogen actually shut off the cortisol that was continually leaking into their bloodstreams, stopping it forever? I can hardly believe it, but here are the test results."

Fascinated, Dara quickly perused the descriptions of the six military vets diagnosed with PTSD, their list of symptoms and the before-and-after results.

"This is more like alternative medicine," Dara finally said. "But you can't argue with the tests and their results."

Excitedly, Alexa said, "I'd really like to schedule a session with Taylor Douglas. I've got my Stearman biplane, and I can fly up there and see her. What do you think, Dara?"

Dara considered Alexa's question. "First, let me read through all this info tonight. Then, I want to put in a call to Ms. Douglas and talk to her myself. Based upon that call, I can let you know what I think." She straightened. "You do know that officially, via the American Medical Association, there is no cure for PTSD. There's nothing out there except sleeping pills and antianxiety medications."

"Yes," Alexa grimaced. "I know. And all those do is suppress the symptoms. They aren't reducing them, Dara. I know I'm not a doctor, nor do I have a medical background, but it looks to me like this adaptogen shuts off the cortisol when the brain's master gland isn't able to accomplish it by itself. And if that's true, according to her other data, the master gland comes back online in that thirty-day period and takes control of the adrenal glands, which manufacture the cortisol. It normalizes how much cortisol is sent out to the person's bloodstream and turns it off as it normally should."

Dara nodded and smiled a little. "If this is true, it's a huge breakthrough. This would help anyone with PTSD symptoms, whether they were in combat or not."

"That's what I was thinking," Alexa murmured, relieved that Dara didn't pooh-pooh the data. She knew many other MDs would discount the information. "Children or adults, for instance, that come out of dysfunctional, abusive homes, or who have been rescued from sex slavery, or who have been traumatized in a hundred different ways, could have their cortisol once more controlled and shut off. They wouldn't have to suffer the horrible anxiety that's with them every day of their lives, preventing them from living normal lives."

"I know," Dara whispered, giving her a sympathetic look. "Well, this all looks very interesting, the data, graphs, and before-and-after results are all here. Doctors need that kind of proof in order to move on it and make an informed decision about it for their patients."

"So you'll let me know what you think?" Alexa needed reassurance.

"I promise, Alexa. I'm hopeful too, but I need to dig into the medical nitty gritty, talk with Taylor Douglas, and see if it all adds up."

"Fingers crossed," Alexa whispered, "that it does. I just have such a powerful, hopeful feeling about this, Dara. I think I'm a prime candidate to try it out."

"I agree. But let's take this a step at a time."

Relief surged through Alexa. "That would be wonderful, Dara. Thank you!" She walked around the desk and gave Dara a hug.

"Keep your hopes up," Dara whispered, smiling and releasing her.

Alexa stepped back and said in an emotional tone, "Gage and I want to start a family, Dara, and I can't do it with the way I feel now. You said pregnancy would intensify my hormonal responses, and if the cortisol is out of control, I'd feel worse than I do now. And I don't know what all these hormones would do to the baby." She wrung her hands. "I don't want to be like this the rest of my life, Dara. If there is anything out there that can help me, I want to try it out. I'm desperate."

Dara slid her arm around Alexa. "I feel so

deeply for you, for what you have to wrestle with daily. I just don't want you going to some alternative medicine person who is promising you something that can't possibly work." She looked deeply into Alexa's strained face. "Okay?"

Dara walked her toward the door after picking up Alexa's briefcase and handing it to her. "You'll hear from me as soon as possible. I promise . . ."

GAGE WALKED INTO their farmhouse after work and spotted Alexa in the kitchen, making them dinner. Going over, he kissed her hello and handed her a bouquet of pink roses wrapped in silver foil with a huge fuchsia ribbon. "For you," he said, watching her expression. It had been a week since she'd seen Dara.

"Ohh, these are so pretty," Alexa said, breathing in the scent of the blooms, then looking up at him with gratitude. "Thank you!" she said, reaching up and sliding her arm around his shoulder, pushing up on her toes and kissing his smiling mouth. Gage wore dark brown corduroys and a long-sleeved white tee that brought out his rugged good looks. To most people, Gage would look pretty ordinary. No one would guess that, as one of the most deadly snipers in Afghanistan, he had saved dozens of

American lives on his watch. He was her everyday hero, and as his mouth met hers, she sank against him, making a joyous sound as his arms pulled her to him.

Coming up for air, Gage reluctantly released her lips, looking at the happiness in her green and gold eyes. Ever since he'd researched Taylor Douglas's website, and Alexa had brought the information to Dara to explore, he'd seen her hopes grow every day.

Gage smiled, moving her tousled hair away from her cheek. "You're the pretty one here," he said. The change in Alexa had been gratifying to Gage, and he prayed that Taylor Douglas was the real deal and that Dara would approve of sending Alexa to her for treatment.

"Mmm, well," she teased him, "if I'm pretty, you are a certified hunk, Gage Hunter."

He smiled, watching the play of gold and green in her widening eyes. Every time she cycled up, he wished with all his heart that she'd remain at that level. That was the way Alexa was before the traumas brought her down again. "Thank you, ma'am. I think you're kinda sexy, and I'm having a hard time deciding whether or not to take you to bed or let you finish up making dinner."

Grinning, she swept her hand across the front of his jeans, feeling just how hard his cock was. "Well, judging from feeling you, big guy, I think the bedroom might be a better idea, huh? We can have dessert before the meal, okay?"

His eyes narrowed as his look changed, and for Alexa, this was one of her favorite moments—when he changed from gentle lover to a powerful hunter who knew what he wanted and intended to take it. It had been four days since the last time they'd made love, and she knew that Gage would never initiate it. Alexa was grateful for his patience with her on this point. One day, she hoped that her old spontaneity would come back, that Gage could haul her into his arms, carry her off to their bed, and take her like the feral animal that lived within him. At those times, he was dangerous, sexual, and intense. He stalked her every time they made love, and that excited her. But the stalking was done with his lips, his teeth, and his body, coaxing her on every level to surrender completely to him. Gage knew how to turn her on, turn up the intensity, and get her fully aroused, taking her beyond her usual warm affection.

The phone rang, and Gage scowled, saying, "Want me to get it?"

"No, I'm closer." Alexa eased out of his arms and set the bouquet on the counter.

Gage's heart skipped a beat when he found out it was Dara calling. And he saw Alexa's expression brighten as she gripped the phone a little tighter, speaking in low tones. Moving around her, Gage took the bouquet and retrieved a tall glass vase, filling it with water, one ear keyed to their conversation. Halfway through it, Alexa gave a little cry, her hand over her mouth. Turning, Gage thought something might be wrong, and he saw that her glistening eyes suddenly swam with tears.

Was it good news or bad? He wasn't sure as he slipped the bouquet into the vase, sensing Alexa closely. God, he hoped it was good news, not bad. All week, Alexa had been focused on what Dara might discover. He walked over, coming up behind her and gently easing her back against the front of himself, wrapping his arms low around her waist, giving her some physical support in case it was bad news.

"Thanks, Dara," Alexa whispered. "I so appreciate you calling us . . ."

Gage felt Alexa tremble as she hung up the phone. She eased out of his embrace and turned around, her gaze locking on his.

"Oh, Gage, I can go!" she announced excitedly. "Dara said she had a long, productive talk with Taylor Douglas about an hour ago." Tears ran down her cheeks and she covered her mouth with her hand, staring up at him.

"That's great," he said thickly, hauling her into his arms. "Go ahead, cry. It's okay." He felt his own eyes grow damp, knowing how much this meant to Alexa. He'd read all the information on Douglas's site and thought it sounded legit, and now Dara had confirmed it.

What if the medication worked for Alexa? What would that mean? Could that adaptogen really shut down the runaway cortisol that her own body couldn't shut down by itself? That would be a miracle to Gage. He'd give his right arm to make that anxiety stop in her, if he could. This adaptogen treatment might just work!

Finally, Alexa quieted in his arms. "Feel better now?" he murmured against her hair, holding her against him.

"M-much," she whispered brokenly. "Oh, Gage, I'm so happy right now I could jump up and down with joy. But at the same time, I'm afraid this won't work for me, that I'll be the oddball who won't respond to it."

"Shh," he whispered, kissing her temple and easing her away from him just enough to engage her darkened eyes. "I have a good feeling about this, Alexa.

"Y-you do?"

"Yup. What did Dara tell you?"

"She said that Taylor is very warm and easy to talk with. She said that she's treated a lot of abused women who were either raped or beaten, with excellent results."

"That's good," Gage agreed. "What else?"

"She said that, the way Dara described my symptoms, I would qualify for the adaptogen treatment. Oh, Gage, I can't believe it! This is the news we've been waiting for!"

He smiled down at her. "Best yet," he agreed "Did Taylor say what her rate of cure was with the adaptogen?"

"She said she's treated a hundred and fifty people. And every one of her patients has responded to it. Those that had severe PTSD would get relief and their anxiety would be alleviated, but sometimes not fully cured. Still, if symptoms are reduced by eighty percent, that means the person can function in normal society again."

"I would think so," Gage agreed. "What about in your case? Did she comment on the symptoms Dara gave her about you?"

"Yes, she said that while she can't guarantee how many of my symptoms will be alleviated, in her other cases involving sexual assaults, most recover completely. She has two patients who did not, but their particular symptoms were seventy percent improved."

"That's great, baby."

"Even if I don't get rid of all my horrible anxiety, it still means I'll be feeling so much more like my old self." She sniffed, wiping the tears off her nose.

"Come on, let's go to our bed," Gage said suddenly. "I just want to hold you for a while." He saw her eyes soften and she nodded, her lower lip still quivering. She had a lot more tears in her to release, and he'd rather hold her on their bed, stretching out, relaxing, and allowing him to fully care for her. Right now Alexa felt so fragile that it almost scared Gage. He'd never felt her like this before and couldn't figure out why now. She had been fragile before, but it had seemed to recede in her since they started living together. Now it was back and even more intense than before.

"Hold on," he murmured, sweeping her up and into his arms. She let out a little cry of surprise, her arms coming around his shoulders. Gage carried her to the bedroom, toeing open the partially cracked door.

Alexa sighed, lying against Gage as he settled her on the bed beside him. His arm was beneath her neck, and he was propped up on his elbow, watching her through half-closed eyes. "Talk to me, baby. What's going on in your head?" Gage smoothed strands away from her face so he could easily see her expression. She lay with her head on his shoulder, her hand resting over his heart.

"A million things," she admitted, her voice husky from crying. "If this works, I can get pregnant, maybe. I need to talk to Taylor about it. I wonder if she's had any experience with women patients who get pregnant after the medicine works? What else does the adaptogen do? Will I always have to take it?"

Gage nodded. These were all good questions.

"According to the literature, it's a one-time deal. You take it for one month, and it's done. I don't ever have to take it again unless I experience a new trauma that might cause the cortisol to get out of control again. Taylor told Dara that with some of her patients, she might have to give them the adaptogen immediately after the new trauma, but only if a saliva test shows that the hormone is out of normal bounds."

"Makes sense," Gage murmured. "What else?" He so desperately wanted this procedure to work for Alexa.

"I want you with me," she whispered, giving him a pleading look. "The weather is too ugly to fly my Stearman to Wind River Airport. Do you think you could get the time off to go with me, Gage? I really need you at my side. You know how my brain is nowadays, how it races and I can't focus. I get distracted so easily."

He tipped her chin up, kissing her salty lips, her breath warm and moist against his face. "I would go to hell and back for you," he rasped against her mouth. "Of course I'll go with you. I'm sure everyone in your family wants this to work for you, and I doubt that Tal will throw a horseshoe if I'm gone for two or three days."

"No," Alexa agreed. "They'll all be so happy to hear this, Gage."

"I'm sure they'll be celebrating, baby." Her

family had a strong psychic connection to one another, and Dilara often said the Turkish side of their family had visionaries, like her grandmother Damia, who'd foreseen Artemis Shipping being the largest shipping company in the world.

"When can we go?" he asked her, eager to get this going.

"I have to call Taylor's office. Dara said that she had a cancellation two days from now and if I wanted, I should call her right away."

"Good," he murmured, sliding his hand down her back, feeling her melt beneath him. "Let's do it."

She sighed and gave him a rueful look. "I'm so glad you'll be going with me, Gage, because right now I feel as if I'm going to break."

Gage knew that when Alexa hit an anxiety high that lasted for days at a time, she was exhausted for an equal amount of time when she came down from it. "Well, maybe that will stop once you get the tests and the doctor gives you that medication."

He could only hope that he was right, and that help was really on the way.

CHAPTER 8

ALEXA COULD BARELY sit still as she and Gage met with Taylor Douglas at her clinic office. Outside, sporadic sun was trying to peek through the snowy gray clouds rolling across the Wind River Valley. To the east were the Salt River Mountains, still covered at the top with snow. Alexa gave Gage a quick, anxious look, but he was sitting back, casual and relaxed while she was fidgeting like a wild horse.

She liked Taylor, whose blue eyes were warm, her voice low and calming. She was about five feet nine inches tall. Alexa admired her sun-streaked blond hair gleaming with highlights. And, best of all, she asked that they call her Taylor, that she was a physician's assistant and didn't need the title doctor, even though some of her patients liked to refer to her with that title. Alexa liked Taylor because she seemed genuine, friendly and low-key.

"Okay," Taylor said, opening up her computer with Alexa's case results in it. "I know you're dying to find out about your cortisol lab test." She turned the computer screen toward them and with a pencil, pointed and said, "Your cortisol is out of normal bounds at eleven a.m. and spikes again at ten p.m. What this means is that you are a candidate for the protocol."

Alexa pressed her hands to her heart in relief. "Oh, thank God," she breathed.

Taylor gave her an understanding look. "With the abnormal spikes at these times, it means that you're most anxious about an hour before lunch. Then the anxiety begins to recede and is back to normal at about five p.m. And then around ten p.m., it goes outside normal limits again. I would think that you have broken sleep until about four a.m., when your cortisol goes back to normal levels. Am I right?"

Gage swallowed convulsively, surprised at the PA's accuracy.

"Yes," Alexa said. "I'm fine in the morning when I get up, but from about eight a.m. through eleven a.m., I can literally feel that anxiety ratcheting upward."

"And you feel most anxious at eleven a.m.?" Taylor asked, making notes as Alexa spoke.

"Yes." Alexa said, "Gage is always worried that I don't eat enough, Taylor, but I keep telling him I'm so jumpy and hyper around noontime, I have no appetite."

"Right," Taylor said. "That's how it works. The anxiety circumvents your hunger. The last thing you want to do is eat at those high cortisol peak times. You simply don't have an appetite. When you're feeling threatened and danger is lurking just around the corner, it is impossible to want food. When you're under threat, your digestion shuts down, and the energy moves over to the perceived or unperceived threat to give you more energy in case you have to fight."

Gage shook his head. "That explains so much," he said gratefully, looking sympathetically at Alexa. She reached out, her hand damp with nervousness. He wrapped it comfortingly into his warm, dry one.

Taylor gave him a kind look, too. "She's lost weight because her cortisol has spiked up. It wasn't that she didn't want to eat, Gage. It was, I suspect, that Alexa's trauma either occurred at around eleven a.m. or ten p.m. When the cortisol spikes at a certain time, it's because the body remembers the trauma it received at that time and the alarm bells go off within."

Drawing in a sharp breath, Alexa looked at Gage. "We were captured near eleven a.m. at that Afghan village. The examination they gave me in that cave was at ten p.m." Alexa pressed her hand to her throat, giving him a stunned look. Gage held her other hand, squeezing it to give her support.

"Then, that's verified," Taylor said. "I'm so sorry this happened to you, Alexa."

"I hope the other women . . . those who had to go through it with me, can receive this information. Maybe it can help them, too."

Leaning back, Taylor said, "Well, let's get you on this adaptogen first." She handed Alexa a large white plastic bottle that contained a thirty-day supply of capsules. "This is a one-month bottle of the medicine you're to take, Alexa. Most people feel their anxiety go away between the third and fourth day. Of course, there are always exceptions, but the anxiety will dwindle down until you feel at peace again. And if it works on you as I hope it does, then you can contact the women who had to go through this brutality with you. Share your experience with them. It's their decision if they want to try this treatment or not. They can come and see me, or they can go to the functional medicine website online. There's a directory of people who are FM specialists who may be closer to where they live."

Gage released Alexa's hand. "Okay," she whispered, holding the bottle, staring at it.

"We decide the prescription on the adaptogen based upon your saliva test results." Taylor tapped the computer screen on Alexa's graph. "Your highest peaks are at these two times. And you are to take one capsule at each of those times. And that's all. Some people think the more you take, the better off you are, but that's not true. The adaptogen has to be given at those critical times, when the cortisol is at its peak. I would love for you to email me the day your anxiety stops, and once it stops, it should not occur again. Okay?"

"Yes," Alexa whispered, touching the bottle. "It just seems so simple. And you said that once I finish my thirty-day supply, I don't have to take it again?"

"That's right," Taylor said, leaning back in her chair and rocking it a bit. "Three months later, my office will send you another saliva test. You'll mail it off to an overnight courier to the lab in Seattle, Washington, and then they'll email me the results. I'll call you, and we'll compare the before-and-after tests. And then I'll know where to go with you at that point."

"What about becoming a mother?" Alexa asked.

"You and I talked about that earlier. What I'd like to do is get your cortisol within normal limits first, and then I feel you should go to your gynecologist to discuss it."

"But . . . can I get pregnant?"

Taylor smiled warmly. "Of course you can. The adaptogen has nothing to do with it. But I strongly counsel you to wait until the anxiety is gone."

"Oh, I will." Alexa gave Gage a huge smile of relief. "Isn't this wonderful?"

"It's a miracle," he agreed quietly.

Taylor nodded somberly. "It really is a miracle. I've seen men and women with lab tests a lot worse than Alexa's. They take the adaptogen, and the anxiety disappears. It doesn't get rid of nightmares or flashbacks, but just getting the anxiety capped and under control by the brain is a huge step toward helping them heal and feel closer to normal."

Gage stirred. "Then why don't more doctors know about this protocol, Taylor? Or the Veteran's Administration?"

Sighing, Taylor said, "Because it's considered an alternative medicine treatment. This country bases its medical intervention on drugs to handle symptoms. Now, an adaptogen isn't a drug, but it can stop the cortisol and the anxiety in anyone. If you're a doctor and you were trained to use the traditional drug system, you probably won't consider nontraditional methods such as herbs, vitamins and minerals, homeopathy, chiropractic, naturopathy, or Eastern medicine. Most MDs weren't taught other ways of helping a patient to heal."

"But you did it," Gage pressed.

"Yes, but I've never been one to rely first on drug medication. I was raised differently," She smiled faintly. "My mother is a microbiologist. She looked into adaptogens for a health food company she works for, and that's how I found out about them, even as a teenager. An adaptogen is a natural substance that helps the body adapt to stress, and it exerts a normalizing effect upon it when needed. A good example of an adaptogen is ginseng root. What you can say about the class of natural adaptogens found out in nature is that they are anti-stress and fatigue fighters. I never took any drugs until I was eighteen and in college, and even then, it was only aspirin. I've seen alternative medicines cure symptoms just as well, or better, than a drug can, because of my mother's work in the herb industry. And medical drugs never cure. They simply suppress the symptom. If you stop taking the drug, the symptoms come back."

Taylor pointed to the bottle Alexa held. "This is a case in point, Gage. Once the cortisol receptors are shut down, the master pituitary gland in our brains takes over the control of the adrenal glands and the hormones it makes and releases into our bloodstream when we need them. The adaptogen gives the master gland a chance to take back control of the adrenal gland's hormones once more. And once it does, you don't need to take the adaptogen again. You've handed the control of hormones back to its natural boss, the pituitary gland. That's as good as it gets."

"I see. But if you're traumatized again, you need to take it again?"

"Right. Sometimes, a person will get into an auto accident. Or an elderly person falls and goes into shock. Trauma is perceived differently by each person's body. And in the cases where high cortisol is running loose and out of control again, I would have you retake the saliva test to check the peak times it's outside normal boundaries. Then I'd give you probably a one or two-week course of the adaptogen once more to shut down the cortisol receptors."

No one wanted this to work more than Gage—except, of course, Alexa.

Taylor sat up and turned the computer screen toward her. "Alexa, I would urge you to go on your three-month sabbatical. You can start taking the adaptogen right now." She held up her wristwatch. "It's eleven a.m. Take your first dose here." She stood and went to a water dispenser, filling a paper cup and walking back to Alexa. "Let's get you some much needed calm."

Giving Taylor a grateful look, Alexa opened the bottle and took out one capsule. In no time, she'd swallowed it and drank the water.

"Take the next one at ten p.m.," Taylor said, smiling as she sat down. "So? Any other questions?"

Alexa looked at Gage. "Do you have any?"

"I do. Will it help Alexa sleep?"

"Usually, once the cortisol is capped and controlled by the pituitary gland in her brain, she'll sleep well. In some patients, it's not a full eight hours, because they might still have nightmares or flashbacks that wake them, but not as often. Everyone gets better sleep," she said. "How much depends upon the individual."

"I'm wondering if I have high cortisol," Gage told Taylor. He hadn't said much about his military past to her. This appointment was for Alexa, and he'd remained silent for the most part, wanting to be a support for her.

"There's only one way to find out, and that's to take the saliva test. I can give you a box, and you can take it home with you. Take the test and send it in. The lab results will be sent to me."

Alexa reached over, her fingers falling across his lower arm. "Do it, Gage. You have some anxiety, too."

"Not as bad as yours," he teased. "But yes, I have anxiety."

"And you were in the military, Gage?"

"Yes, I was." Gage didn't want to elaborate. "Let me take the box home with us, and I'll give it a whirl."

Taylor nodded and smiled a little. "Sounds good." She directed her attention to Alexa. "Remember, contact me by phone or email once your anxiety tamps down."

"Oh, you'll be the second person I contact," Alexa said, hopeful. "Gage will be the first to know. He's so sensitive to my mood changes, he'll probably know before I do."

TAL AND MATT dropped by for a visit four days later. It was a late Saturday morning., the sky a bright blue, the air chilly. Alexa wasn't expecting her sister and brother, but was happy to see them. Gage was out back at the small barn, working.

Tal grinned as she stepped into the kitchen after stomping snow off her feet on the mud porch rug.

"Hey, Matt and I were slumming in the neighborhood and thought we'd unexpectedly drop in."

Alexa grinned and came over, hugging her tall older sister. Tal wore jeans, work boots, and a red sweater beneath her heavy gray wool coat. "Come on in. What a nice surprise!"

Matt entered and shut the door behind him, shrugging out of his black leather jacket and dark green knit muffler. "Hey, baby sister, you're looking better," he said, and he moved around Tal as she hung up her coat on a nearby wooden hook.

Alexa closed her eyes, hugging her twin, inhaling the fresh, clean air around him. "I've missed you, too." Since deciding not to go to Artemis on weekends, she'd seen a lot less of them. That was something she missed terribly. Releasing Matt, she said, "Would you two like some coffee? We can sit at the kitchen table and chat."

"Yeah," Matt said, looking around. "Where's Gage? I didn't see him when we drove in."

"He's out in the barn. That's what we get for wanting a wood-burning fireplace. Every Saturday is wood chopping day for the coming week."

"I'll go out and see him, give him a hand," Matt said. He gave Tal an evil grin. "I suspect the girl talk will drive me out of here, anyway."

Punching him playfully in the upper arm, Alexa muttered, "You men! You're all alike. Fine, go see Gage. It isn't like you don't see him five days a week at Artemis."

"Yeah," he said, grabbing his jacket and muffler. "But I can keep him company out there and we can talk football while we work."

Rolling her eyes, Alexa shook her head. "Get out of here, twin."

Matt leaned over, kissing her hair. "We'll grab some coffee with you in a while."

Tal poured coffee for Alexa and herself and carried it to the table, sitting down. "Matt and I were dying to find out how that appointment with the functional medicine specialist in Wyoming went," she said, sliding a mug over toward Alexa.

Alexa pushed her hair off her shoulders and sat down at Tal's left elbow. "Well, I'm afraid to say anything yet," she said. "But this morning I woke up and I felt calmer. Usually, my PTSD ramps up to high at eleven a.m."

"And?" Tal coaxed, sipping her coffee, watching her closely.

Shrugging, Alexa whispered unsteadily, "I don't have the anxiety at this time today, Tal. Honest to God, I don't." She took in a ragged breath. "And I'm afraid to tell Gage. I'm afraid it won't last. Or that it's my imagination." She curved her hands around the bright yellow ceramic cup.

Tal nodded, reaching out, gripping her shoulder. "That's good news."

"It will be if it lasts, Tal. I'm just not sure. I'm shaky about it."

"Well, I'll stay mum," she promised. "You know, you don't look as tired as before. Are you sleeping a little better?"

"Yeah," she mumbled. "Last night, I slept all night through. I never realized what sleep deprivation does to you until you feel good again from a solid eight hours under your belt."

"I don't see shadows under your eyes like I usually do," Tal said, smiling a little, holding

Alexa's concerned gaze.

"Taylor said it would sneak up on me. That I wouldn't realize it until that gnawing anxiety wasn't there the way I expected it to be. The sleep is a blessing, let me tell you."

"But the anxiety? It's completely gone?"

"Today is the first day," Alexa admitted, frowning. "It's like someone shut off a faucet inside me. I feel the way I used to before I was captured by the Taliban. I'm calm, and I even feel more like my confident old self." She flashed Tal an uneasy smile.

"Wow!" Tal murmured. "I never realized that medicine could do so much for you so fast."

"Well, let's just wait and see, okay? I'm on pins and needles because the anxiety is gone, and I'm worried it's going to come back and hit me hard."

"I can imagine you're jumpy about it." Tal gave her a sympathetic look. "Are you and Gage getting ready to fly to the Keys? I was talking to Mom earlier this morning, and she said she's baking up some of your favorite Turkish food to take with you." She grinned. "I think Mom should start a catering business on the side." They both chuckled.

"I'm packing, and so is Gage," Alexa said, gesturing down the hall toward their open bedroom door. "We've got a ways to go yet."

"When will you fly the Stearman down

there?"

"Andy, my mechanic, and I have some stuff to attend to. Mechanical inspections. We might leave two or three days from now . . ."

"You are a grease monkey, no doubt," Tal said, smiling as she sipped her coffee.

Alexa held up her hands. Her fingernails were short and she pointed to them. "I've been out there two days in a row with Andy, and I can't get the grease out from beneath my nails."

"Well, you're the one who likes hands-on mechanical stuff," Tal drawled.

"I know. I think I got my mechanics gene from Dad."

"For sure. When he's home, he's always out in the garage tinkering with the lawn mower, the weed whacker, or anything else he can get his hands on," Tal grinned.

"Well, come March, I've got to have my hands looking nice," Alexa said.

"How are the wedding plans coming along?" Tal asked, seeing her sister's eyes alight with happiness.

"I told Mom yesterday that I was going to look at the booklets from several fashion designers and take them with me to the Keys. I want Gage to look at them with me, too."

"That will be nice," Tal agreed. "Mom's already got a couple picked out for you, like she does for me."

She and Gage were to be married in March. And then, Matt and Dara were going to be married at Uncle Ihsan's villa in Kuşadası come June. Tal and Wyatt's wedding was going to take place is Kuşadası, Turkey, in August. It was certainly a year like no other—all three of them would be married, which Alexa found amazing and wonderful.

Smiling fondly, Tal said, "I think it's incredible that all of us are getting married in the same year. Could you look back on our lives and see something like this happening? What are the odds?" She opened her hands, shaking her head.

"Hey, we met men who are incredible," Alexa said. "Gage is such a hero to me."

"Wyatt's a royal pain in my ass at times, but I do love him despite his Texas 'go big or go home' attitude," Tal drawled, chuckling.

Giggling, Alex agreed. "Matt has the nicest woman in the world who loves him. Dara is just so kind and gentle."

"He *really* got lucky," Tal agreed, giving Alexa a mischievous look. "It never hurts to have a doctor in the family. The next thing that will happen is that everyone will become fertile myrtles at the same time, mark my words. We do things in triplicate around here."

Alexa sighed. "I so want to settle down, Tal. I want a family. I hunger for it."

"How does Gage feel about it?"

"He's worried about my anxiety and PTSD. If this adaptogen works, Taylor said I should take three months and then talk to a gynecologist about getting pregnant."

"That sounds pretty reasonable to me. Is Gage ready for fatherhood?"

Alexa knew that Tal was aware that Gage had lost his family when he was young. "Yes, we've discussed it a number of times. He's more than ready."

"He'll make a good father," Tal agreed quietly.

"His dad was a great role model for Gage, and I'm sure he'll pass that on to our children."

Tal said, "I was thinking, maybe, just maybe, you'll end up loving motherhood and family so much, you won't want to work at Artemis anymore."

Alexa knew that Tal was an excellent judge of character and had deep insights into people. "I was thinking the same thing, Tal. Gage thinks I should stay away from the Safe House Foundation, that it brings up too many memories and upsets me too much right now."

"I agree with him," Tal murmured.

"Could you get along without me, Tal?"

Tal gave her a fond look. "Well, you won't be very far away from us, Alexa. No matter what you want to do, my instinct is that you were made for motherhood, and that you and Gage will have a bunch of kids. I think what's happened to you may have moved your life course in another direction, but I believe it's going to play to another strength of yours: being maternal, loving children, and wanting to be a mother. That's always been there in you, big time. You were the one that always wanted to play with dolls, not me." Tal grinned.

Alexa nodded. "You're right, Tal. I've always wanted a big family, like Mom's Turkish family. I love the warmth between all our relatives."

"Well," Tal murmured, finishing off her coffee, "I can see you and Gage with three kids for sure. He lost his family, and yours could be a replacement family for him, a starting-over. A nice one. The guy deserves some good things to happen to him after his lousy start in life."

"He deserves so much happiness," Alexa said, her eyes tearing up.

"He's good for you, Alexa, and he has rare qualities of honor, integrity, and kindness in his bones."

Alexa wiped her eyes. "Gosh, all of sudden I'm so teary."

"Could it be that the adaptogen is working?"

"I don't know. It could be. I'm not feeling numbed out like I usually do. My emotions seem to be on tap within me again, and I think that's a good sign."

"Are you still calm inside?" Tal looked at her

watch. "It's noon."

"I still do. It's so wonderful, Tal, I can hardly believe it. I'm beginning to feel a tiny bit like I did before all that trauma."

Tal smiled warmly. "I think it's a miracle. Mom's brothers have been going to their mosque to pray for you every day since you were kidnapped. That's pretty significant."

"Yes, Uncle Ishan emailed me when I told them I was on this adaptogen." Her voice lowered, and she sniffed. "I don't care what the religion is, Tal. If you're praying from your heart for someone else, it works."

"You'll get no argument from me," Tal said. She heard the back door open and the tramping of feet, then the door closing. "Sounds like Matt and Gage have arrived. Can I help you in the kitchen and we'll make lunch?"

Smiling, Alexa stood. "Sure can. Lucky for us all, we just roasted a turkey breast yesterday. Turkey sandwiches sound good?"

Tal rose. "Yep, they sure do."

CHAPTER 9

ALEXA STRETCHED OUT her naked body against Gage as they settled into bed for the night. They had made love in the shower once again, and her body glowed from the unexpected session. Then Gage had washed her hair as she sat on the warm marble bench, the water cascading over her shoulders and back. She relished when he washed and then brushed her hair.

Nuzzling his jaw, Alexa whispered, "I need to share something with you."

Gage had seen how restless Alexa had been all afternoon. She enjoyed seeing her brother and sister, but there was something else going on that he couldn't figure out. He moved to his side, propping himself up on an elbow to look at her more closely. For their shower, she had piled her hair up on her head with gold barrettes. Now he eased both of them from her hair and placed them on the bed stand.

"Are you feeling okay? You seemed a little restless today," he said, trying not to sound concerned.

"Well," she whispered, frowning, "I just wanted to make sure."

One corner of his mouth hitched. He skimmed his hand across her belly. "Sure about what?" He saw Alexa lick her lower lip, a sure sign of something important about to be said.

"The adaptogen, Gage. I think it's working." She saw his eyes widen, and his hand stilled on her belly.

"What level of anxiety are you at?"

She smiled softly. "Ever since I woke up this morning, I've felt no anxiety, Gage. None! I can't believe it." She rested her hand over his, feeling his concern, mixed with hope, for her words. "I told Tal about it at noon, how afraid I was that it would come back to slam me."

"And you're taking two capsules a day?"

Nodding, she released a fragmented sigh, frowning. "I-I didn't believe Taylor when she said it would just shut off. Yesterday, I had anxiety. Today, nothing." She slid her hand up across his chest, his skin moist beneath her fingertips. "And tonight, when we made love in the shower . . ."

"Yes?"

"It was . . . well . . . different."

"How do you mean?" He tried to keep the trepidation out of his voice. Gage saw how tentative Alexa was right now and knew how badly she wanted this protocol to work.

"Well, before my capture, orgasms were very intense, when I had one. I mean, I felt near to fainting sometimes, Gage, the pleasure was that profound." She lifted her lashes, staring up at him. "Tonight, I almost fainted. It felt like the kind of orgasm I used to have before the capture."

Gage leaned down, kissing her lips. "Then it's working, baby. Taylor said less than a week, and you've been on them four days now."

She made a small sound, sliding her hand through his damp hair. "But I'm afraid, Gage, that it will come back."

"Taylor said it wouldn't," he reminded her quietly. "She said it was like a faucet being shut off, and last night, I watched as you slept so damned hard, Alexa, better than I've seen. Maybe that's part of the proof that the adaptogen is working." He teased a few damp strands of her auburn hair that were stuck against her cheek and slid them behind her ear.

Alexa pulled him down upon her, burying her face against his neck. "Oh, I hope you're right, Gage. I want this so bad . . ."

Hearing the fear in her voice, he kissed her hair and said reassuringly, "It's happening, baby.

Maybe you should call Taylor tomorrow?"

"Oh, I can't. It's Sunday, Gage."

He grunted. "Okay, Monday then." Moving Alexa into his arms, he leaned against the headboard, bringing her into his embrace. "Does it feel like you used to feel before being captured?" he asked, holding her gaze.

"Yes. The same. I'm quiet inside, Gage. I can't explain it. It's like this invisible animal with teeth had been eating me from the inside out. Then, suddenly, it's gone. Just . . . gone . . ."

He murmured, "If you wake up tomorrow morning and you're still feeling quiet and calm inside . . ."

"Yes?"

"Then it's for real, Alexa. I think you can take it to the bank."

She pressed her face against his chest. "Oh, Gage, I want it to be! I so want it to be . . ."

He rocked her a little, feeling how worried she was right now. "Right after my dad and Jen got murdered, I used to go to bed at night and hope that when I woke up in the morning, they'd be out at the kitchen table—Dad with his coffee, Jen with her Cheerios. I think in your case, this is real. It's working. And it's here to stay."

Never had Alexa wanted to hear anything more than that. Gage felt so solid, so stable, and was ultimately practical.

"Believe me, I understand how you could

feel that way, Gage. It breaks my heart that you had to go through that alone."

"Hey," he groused, "I didn't bring it up to make you feel bad. I'm just showing you how our minds and emotions can skew us sideways at times."

"My mind is still churning, Gage. I'm not thinking as logically as I usually do," she admitted.

"Maybe that will go away, too," he suggested.

Alexa closed her eyes as he caressed her cheek with his rough palm. "I'm so tired of fighting it, Gage. To wake up this morning and feel nothing but this delicious calm throughout me—I felt as if I'd died and gone to heaven. And the more I woke up, the more I realized that the monster wasn't prowling around inside me anymore. I kept watching the clock, thinking it would wake up again." She swallowed hard. "But it didn't . . . it hasn't . . . yet."

FOR THE LONGEST time, Gage lay on his back with Alexa curled up beside him, sleeping deeply. Allowing her to talk out her fears always seemed to calm her. They'd had great sex in the shower, the best he could remember. And maybe, just maybe, that damned cortisol had been turned off by the adaptogen. God, he hoped so.

In the next two days, they would be getting ready to fly to the Keys. Alexa was always happy, always in her element, when she was out at the hangar with her Stearman biplane. Her mechanic, Andy, in his fifties, gray-bearded with a twinkle in his green eyes, was like a doting uncle to her. They'd work together on the plane, their wooden toolboxes with all kinds of wrenches, pliers, screwdrivers, and work gloves nearby as they tinkered with the ancient engine until it fired on all pistons, the sound making them smile for a job well done.

Closing his eyes, Gage envisioned Alexa when she'd first met him at the canteen at Bagram. She'd been like blinding sunlight to his dark, fractured soul. Her broad smile had fed him hope and made him want to capture that sunbeam brilliance she radiated. It was like capturing fireflies in a Mason jar. He knew he couldn't, but to sit there at that table with her and her brother, Matt, all of them eating pizza and drinking beer, had changed his life.

At lunch today, Gage had enjoyed the sibling repartee between the three of them. Alexa began to shine once more, as she had upon first meeting him. The sunlight was back in her eyes, the green and gold flecks prominent, the sienna nearly nonexistent. The warmth, camaraderie, and love between the three siblings made Gage ache for Jen and his family, but he hid it well, interacting with all of them, sharing laughs and jokes. Yet his heart yearned for what had been cruelly ripped away from him.

Alexa wanting to become a mother meant more to Gage than he'd admitted to her, and it was something he needed to sit down and share with her. His desire for family drove him whether he realized it or not. Until he'd met Alexa, it hadn't been a clear thought or a need, but it was turning into a deep longing. He'd had his family torn from him, and there would be no more photos of them, no more shared memories.

But once Alexa was pregnant, he knew his life would truly change. It was so important to his soul and heart, a possibility he could hang onto, that lately he could think of little else but seeing Alexa with a belly huge with his child. Gage now understood how much his father had loved his mother. As a child, what did he know or realize? Not much. But he remembered how his father looked when he came home from deployment, the deep adoration Gage saw in his father's eyes for his mother. And he always touched his wife with warmth, tenderness, and appreciation. They had that kind of rare, wonderful marriage.

And now, Gage was living with a woman he would marry next March, and he would give her his heart because she deserved nothing less from him. Gage was filled with so much hope, but he knew it hinged on the success of the cortisol protocol.

Gradually, Gage's lids fell closed. Alexa was in his embrace, her head nestled trustingly on his shoulder, her soft, curvy body resting beside his hard planes. Now he began to worry about the enemies of Delos, and the blood revenge against the families as a whole.

They'd barely dodged a bullet when Rasari went undercover and assumed another identity. Gage believed he was more dangerous than Zakir Sharan, but both men had lost sons to Matt and Tal over in Afghanistan. Tal had a team putting together a PSD, personal security detail plan, for the entire global family. Robert Culver, especially, felt the whole family was at risk, not just the American contingent. And if that was so, there were a lot of Turkish and Greek young adults at risk, too. Gage wasn't sure how the adult children would react to the information, but he knew that Uncle Ihsan and Dilara's other two brothers, Berk and Serkan, took it with dead seriousness.

There were a lot of balls in the air right now. Because Gage had been a sniper and was in black ops, he'd told Tal and the planning team that he didn't want a security contractor shadowing their every move. He'd handle it on his own and felt confident about doing so.

Alexa did not have her head in the game, but Gage didn't expect it to be. Until she could get this cortisol under control, she was completely distracted in every way. And even if the adaptogen worked, when they returned from the Keys, Gage would buy a trained guard dog for their farmhouse. To outsiders, the dog would appear to be just a dog. But he'd be much more. He didn't want Alexa alone in their home without one to warn her when someone drove into the driveway. She'd fallen apart the other day when the electric company man had shown up at their property unannounced. No, there was no question: they needed a dog. That was the last thought he had as he drew in a deep, slow breath, Alexa's rose fragrance filling his lungs.

THE YELLOW, RED, and white Boeing PT-17A Stearman biplane gleamed in the bright overhead sunlight the next day at Potomac Airfield. Andy was with Alexa, who had her sunglasses on, her hair up, a shirt over her sleeveless tee, carrying a huge, weighty wrench across her shoulders. Andy was doing a final FAA inspection on the World War I biplane. It was one of the few Stearmans to be equipped with blind-flying instrumentation, meaning Alexa could fly in IFR, instrument flight rules, for poor visibility conditions. Without that equipment on board, she could only fly as far as she could see visually. She could never take off in fog conditions, low visibility, or heavy cloud conditions. With the valuable instruments on board, her little biplane could be flown day or night. It had canvas skin stretched and painted on the upper and lower wings, its huge engine clean and prepped for tomorrow's flight to the Keys.

Gage acted as a gofer for the two of them as they chatted, laughed, and worked on the Continental R-670-5 seven-cylinder air-cooled radial engine together. Alexa got all excited about her little plane's capabilities. It had a 220-horsepower engine, cruised at 96 mph, and had a service ceiling for 13,200 feet. And then she wickedly said that she had no oxygen masks in the cockpit, and she'd always fly below ten-thousand feet because of that. He'd laughed. The Stearman, when the throttle was applied to it, could go as fast as 135 mph. Not fast, in Gage's opinion. But, as Alexa pointed out, if the engine died midair, they could easily float to the ground and probably land unscathed, whereas in today's domestic jet airliners, they wouldn't coast at all because they were too heavy, much harder to land without killing everyone on board. He didn't pretend to know an aircraft engine, but Alexa clearly did, because excitement burned in her eyes as she went through an alphabet soup Gage couldn't really follow. She was clearly impressed with the engine on her biplane. Andy treated her like a much-loved niece. He was dressed in a pair of denim overalls, a dark blue polo shirt with the sleeves pushed up, and a dark blue baseball cap on his flyaway silver hair.

Potomac Airfield sat in Fort Washington, Maryland, a twenty-five-minute drive from Alexandria. Alexa did not want to use busy Reagan National Airport near Washington, D.C. This particular airfield had eighty-seven aircraft on it—eighty-four were single engine, like her Stearman. There were a number of World War II aircraft that Gage had seen too, like P-51 Mustangs, Navy F4U Corsairs, and Army trainers. It was a busy little airport with planes from the past.

Now they had pushed the biplane out of a huge aluminum hangar and onto the concrete, because the November day felt like September and the temperature was in the mid-sixties. The sun felt good beating down on the shoulders of Gage's lightweight nylon jacket, a black t-shirt beneath it. He wore a black baseball cap on his head, plus wraparound sunglasses. Even though Alexa swore that this tiny one-runway airport was safe, he took nothing for granted. Under his jacket, he carried a Glock pistol in a holster at the small of his back, hidden to prying eyes by the fabric hanging down over his hips.

It was a perfect time to come out here, an Indian summer day, because snow had already fallen and now warm weather followed. All the trees outside the cyclone fenced-in airport area were naked and without leaves. As Gage walked around, some of his hearing was keyed to Andy and Alexa, his other ear listening for anything that sounded out of place for the area. He was in complete sniper mode. As much as he wished he could relax and lounge around, now was not the time or place to do that.

No one knew what Rasari or Sharan were up to or where they might try to strike next.

Gage wanted to celebrate that Alexa had awakened this morning anxiety-free. She was dying to call Taylor the next morning, Monday, to share what had happened to her. Today, she seemed less worried about the anxiety coming back. In fact, she looked and felt more settled than he'd seen her since the capture. It was as if she were slowly accepting that the medication might be working.

Gage had his fingers crossed. Alexa had slept ten hours, and he'd awakened her at ten a.m. She looked and acted drugged the first hour, but he'd gotten two cups of strong Turkish coffee into her that helped her wake up. It was a perfect day, except for the possibility of being attacked by their enemies.

Would it be in the Keys? He might be able to relax, but probably not. Enemies struck when their quarry was relaxed, not vigilant.

★

GAGE WAS AT Artemis on Monday, getting ready to go down to the cafeteria for lunch when Alexa burst into his office. Her face was radiant, her eyes shining. She wore a pair of camel-colored wool slacks, a vest of the same material with a ruffled orange silk blouse beneath her gray wool coat. Her auburn hair was down in a shining cloak around her shoulders, her expression joyous.

"Hey," he called, getting up from his desk and going around it to meet her. "Did you call Taylor?" She had been preparing to do so when Gage had left for work this morning. There was a two-hour difference in time zones, so Alexa had to wait until it was nine a.m. in Wyoming to make that call. When they'd gotten up this morning, Alexa was still feeling calm, and every day, she looked more hopeful of getting her life back.

"Gage!" and she threw herself into his opening arms, crushing him with a hug. "Taylor said it's working!"

He absorbed her full weight, taking a step back to steady himself. Gripping her to him, he hugged her fiercely. "That's great," he murmured, kissing her hard.

Alexa pulled back, smiling radiantly. "She said it won't come back, that the adaptogen has shut down the cortisol receptors. Isn't that wonderful, Gage?" She choked, fighting back tears.

"Yes, that's the best news yet, baby." Gage wanted to kiss the hell out of her, but there were people moving up and down the hall who could look in and see them. He had to practice *some* restraint, so he kissed her brow and drank in the green and gold of her eyes. She was so happy, and therefore, so was he.

"What else did Taylor say?" he asked.

"That I'll continue to feel calm and have no more anxiety. I should stay on the regimen for the full thirty days, and that's all." Sighing, Alexa said, "I just can't believe this, Gage. It was that simple, and yet ninety-nine percent of the military vets and abuse survivors don't know about this alternative protocol. They're suffering horribly when they don't have to suffer at all. How sad is that?"

Gage nodded and released her. "Until the traditional medical establishment accepts alternative medicine protocol, they'll refuse to use it. And that's even sadder. I thought medicine, any type of medicine, was about healing the person, not that it had to fit a certain philosophical model in order to be used."

"Hey," Alexa said, "I'm going to find Tal and Matt to tell them."

"No need," Gage said, "We're all meeting down in the cafeteria for lunch. Want to come along?" He slid his arm around her waist.

"Oh, yes!"

★

GAGE SAT BACK at the long white table, trays of food sitting on it. Tal and Matt were ecstatic about what had happened to Alexa. Excitement sizzled between the three siblings, and Gage smiled to himself as he ate his salad. Alexa could hardly sit still next to him, squirming around, her hands flying all over the place as she shared the story of what had happened to her with the adaptogen.

"Well," Tal said after hearing the whole story, sliding a glance towards Matt on her left, "I don't give a damn what traditional medical doctors say about it. We need to hire a functional medicine specialist for Artemis. Everyone here, more or less, has PTSD symptoms. If we can delete the anxiety, which I feel is the biggest daily issue for some of our employees, it will be worth every penny in the long run. And we need to use this protocol throughout our Safe House Foundation Charities, as well. I'll talk to Mom about it."

"I'm sure Taylor could help us," Alexa suggested, rubbing her hands together, thoroughly excited.

Tal said, "Can you send her an email when you get home? Tell her our needs. I'd like to hire her as a consultant to help us set up a charity-wide plan and protocol. I'd also like to have a medical person around here, because our people are going to get PTSD, no question. We've got good medical insurance, and if traditional medical insurance companies won't accept it, we'll pay for it out of pocket. Our employees deserve this. I've seen what the anxiety has done to you, Alexa, and I wouldn't wish that plague on anyone."

Soberly, Alexa said, "I'm seriously thinking of writing some blogs on it. Or an article. Something. Because people have to know about this protocol. It could literally save lives. I mean, I've read of vets who have such bad anxiety, they commit suicide. It's their only escape. That's how bad it is."

Grimly, Tal said," Well, none of our employees are going to be hung out to dry like that. We'll get an FM trained person in here to treat them. Besides, taking antianxiety medication or prescription sleeping pills only goes so far. And some people feel worse, not better."

Matt said, "I like this. I'm going to contact Taylor this afternoon and ask for that saliva test she gave you, Gage."

"I just turned my saliva samples to the lab, and they'll go through my results," he said. "I'm hoping to hear later this week from Taylor as to whether or not my cortisol is out of normal bounds."

"Do you have anxieties, Gage?" Tal asked him.

"Some." He shrugged. "But I have broken sleep from nightmares. And Taylor said that's one of the symptoms of anxiety caused by cortisol being out of normal bounds. I'm hopeful that if my test results come back high, she can prescribe the adaptogen for me. I'd like to sleep eight hours a night. I don't know what that's like anymore."

Tal grimaced. "Well, I don't sleep throughout the night, either. Maybe I should take the test."

"I think you should," Alexa pleaded, reaching over, gripping Tal's hand. "I've slept eight hours a night for the last three nights, Tal. I can't tell you how good I feel now! I have more energy, I'm hopeful again, and I'm starting to get my appetite back."

Gage cut her a wry look. "Maybe now I won't have to force feed you," he teased, his mouth hooking into a grin.

Laughing lightly, Alexa threw her arm around his shoulders, kissing his cheek and then releasing him. "Hey, I'm on vacation for the next three months! I don't think you'll have to beg me to eat. Besides, I love fish and all the other seafood that's going to be available to us in the Keys."

"I'm so damned jealous," Tal told her. "I love our Keys winter house. It's nice to go down there, because it's so much warmer than the snow country we have here."

"Well," Alexa suggested, "why don't you and

Wyatt, Matt, and Dara plan to fly down for a weekend? That house has ten bedrooms, more than enough for all of us."

"Maybe we'll get Mom and Dad to come down with us," Matt suggested. "Kind of make it a family affair? I'm sure they'd like to see how you're doing from time to time, Alexa."

"Yes," Alexa agreed, "That's a great idea!" She turned to Gage. "Would you be all right with our family descending upon us?"

He chuckled. "Sure. My sense is to do it maybe in a month, to give you about four weeks just to be quiet and heal?"

"Yeah," Tal murmured, giving her an evil look. "You do know what will happen, don't you, Alexa? The moment our mother tells our Turkish uncles and wives, and Cousin Angelo and Maria from Greece, they'll all want to fly in like a flock of geese to be with us, too."

"Ohh," Alexa said. "You're right."

Gage gave Tal a puzzled look. "They'd do that?"

Matt smiled. "Oh, you don't know the half of it, Gage, but you will. You're marrying Alexa, so you're going to get immersed in this American-Turkish-Greek family that's invisibly tied to one another. If there's a party somewhere in the world among the family, the entire family flies in to be with them," he laughed.

"Don't forget," Tal told them, "that Mom

and Dad usually visit the Keys winter homestead in January or February, when the snow is at its worst up here in Virginia. And the Turkish and Greek components of our family fly in for about two weeks and stay with them down in the Keys."

"Yes," Matt said dryly, "a moveable party feast is ongoing."

"But," Alexa said, suddenly worried, "it's November. And you know? Mom and Dad's house is where the family is going to have Christmas this year."

"Maybe," Tal suggested, "you should take the four weeks you need and then fly north to celebrate Christmas with all of us. Then you can fly back to the Keys afterward."

"Even better," Matt said, resting his elbows on the table, "is if everyone could fly down to the Keys winter home after Christmas to celebrate New Year's down there." He glanced over at Alexa. "Do you think you could handle that kind of stress and fun?"

"I'm stress-free right now," Alexa shot back.

Gage placed his hand behind Alexa's chair, his heart swelling with relief and love for her. He couldn't believe his eyes. This was the old Alexa he'd met at the canteen in Bagram. When Alexa was fully engaged with life, not being derailed and distracted by that gnawing anxiety, she took his breath away. Could he really have Alexa back as she was before the capture? Gage knew he'd have to take it day by day, and so would she. He caught her dancing hazel gaze and smiled over at her, curving his hand around her shoulder, giving her a small squeeze of support.

Now, he was looking forward to the sabbatical for Alexa at the Keys winter home. What new adventures would they get into? Gage didn't for a second forget that their enemies were stalking the family, and he would quietly remain on guard for himself and Alexa while down there.

Tal and Matt were already locking a security plan into place for the entire global family right now. Gage was actively working on implementing that plan today until he left with Alexa for the Florida Keys. Even then, he would be in touch with Artemis and the planners to ensure it was fully in place within the next two weeks, no matter where he was. Gage would be carrying a sat phone on him and his Toughbook laptop too, as well as many other electronic devices that would keep him in the heartbeat of Artemis.

Matt groaned. "I can just see this now," he told them, folding his hands behind his head, grinning like a fool. "Mom doesn't know it, but the whole family will descend a week before Christmas at their home and then stay over for longer than she was expecting."

"Oh, pooh!" Alexa said. "Mom will love it!"

"Dad will probably retire to his man cave in

the basement," Matt chuckled.

Gage grinned. "I may join him."

Alexa elbowed him in the ribs. "Gage! You'll love our big family. Really. Give them a chance, okay?"

"Yeah, do," Tal intoned, giving Matt a dark look. "Dad isn't Turkish or Greek, and he can't take the party atmosphere twenty-four hours a day. But you may find certain family members that you really warm up to, Gage. They're intelligent people, every one of them. And kind. And yes, they do love to celebrate and enjoy life to the fullest, but maybe they can teach you how to see life in a more fun, hopeful way, too."

"Point taken," Gage agreed, giving Tal a slight smile. "I just have a tough time seeing you in party mode, though, Tal."

Alexa snickered and Matt laughed outright.

Tal's black eyebrows went down. "I know how to party," she said indignantly.

"Yes," Alexa said. "You have to remember; Tal is a Capricorn."

"Is that another word for stick-in-the-mud?" Matt inquired sweetly, tugging at Tal's ponytail.

"Get out of here," Tal growled at Matt. "I know how to party! And I'm not a stick-in-the-mud. I do have to be serious when things are serious, but when our whole family gets together, I'm partying right along with everyone else. We all have Turkish and Greek blood in our veins, little brother."

Matt pounded his chest. "Wounded by my big sister! Arghh . . ."

Gage laughed at Matt's sudden, unexpected antics. Usually, he was as low-key and quiet and serious as Tal. This was the first time he'd seen Matt cut loose, and it was telling. Alexa giggled and Tal chuckled.

"Matt Culver," Tal said with a straight face, "you're such a clown when you want to be."

Matt gave Tal an amused look, straightening up in his chair. "And you wouldn't ever think of being one. Right?"

"Yeah," Matt offered, giving Tal a teasing look. "And I have it on video."

Tal colored. "Now . . . don't you dare show Gage that video, Matt, or I'll strangle you!"

Alexa turned to Gage. "Three years ago, Tal really cut loose after Christmas dinner over in Athens. I think it was too much retsina wine, but she was dancing on tabletops with Cousin Angelo."

"Really?" Gage said, giving Tal a shocked look. Tal was always the quiet, responsible one, from what he'd seen so far.

"Really," Matt said. "I got it on video." And then he snickered. "It's a family heirloom now, you know? Tal's always so serious, but on that day, Cousin Angelo got her up on that long banquet table when the Greek band started playing, and she was quite a sight, believe me."

Gage felt sorry for Tal. He'd never seen her blush, but she was doing it now. Tal was an introvert, like him. He didn't know if he was a Capricorn or not, but he understood quiet, introverted people because he was one himself. "Hey, Tal," he said, getting her attention. "I'm with you on this one. I'm not gonna be found dancing on any tabletops either."

Tal grinned. "My baby brother threatens to put my wild-haired episode on YouTube some-day, but so far, he's protected my back. Haven't you, Matt?" She slid him a wicked look.

"Yeah, I wouldn't do that to you," he admitted, smiling. "It's a black ops thing, you know? We don't put photos of us out there for our enemies to see, so that video is safe. But—" he waved his finger toward Tal "—I still think Gage and Wyatt would really enjoy seeing it, don't you?"

"Not on my watch," Tal growled warningly. "You show that to Wyatt and you're dead meat. Certified, Culver."

Alexa chortled. "This is where you see our big sister put her foot down," she told Gage merrily.

"Yeah," Tal said, "but I mean it."

"She does, too," Alexa said, giving Tal a warm look. She reached out, gripping her older sister's hand. "You *know* we wouldn't show that video unless you gave us permission."

"I can be bribed," Matt said, gloating smugly over at Tal.

"What? You want some M&M's?" Tal demanded, giving him a sour smile.

"That would probably do it," Matt agreed amiably.

Gage sat back, listening to the siblings tease the hell out of each other. But it wasn't mean teasing or hurtful. It reminded him so much of himself, Jen, and his parents. They'd start ribbing one another at the dinner table. The Culvers' teasing made him feel even more a part of this global family he would soon marry into.

Of the three siblings, Alexa was like brilliant sunshine. Gage looked upon Matt as being a summer day. And Tal was a moonlit, star-filled night. Each of the grown children was a unique individual bound by powerful ties of love. There was no maliciousness between any of them. And clearly, they fit right in with their big, global family, warts and all.

"I, for one," Alexa said, as they broke up to go back to their offices after lunch, "am really looking forward to Christmas and New Year's."

"You'd better call Mom and tell her what's going down," Tal warned her. "You know she doesn't like surprises like this. It will take her all of November to get things set up for the family to descend upon their two homes."

"No worries," Alexa said breezily, hooking her arm through Gage's arm. "When I go home, I'll call Mom."

Gage walked with the family to the elevators down the hall from the cafeteria dining room. "Will she be happy about this?" he asked Alexa.

"Oh, for sure," Alexa said. "Mom's Turkish with a smidgen of Greek thrown in. Any day is a party day for her. Any excuse will do."

Tal hit the elevator button. "Only Mom is the kind of person who wants a warning so she can organize the whole thing, first. I know she isn't expecting to fly down to the Keys for New Year's with everyone."

"Yeah," Alexa agreed. "But they have employees who take care of the house, so I think the biggest thing is just getting it organized."

The elevator doors opened. Tal stepped in with Matt, followed by Gage and Alexa. She hit the button for the fifth floor. "I hope Dad will be able to come to the Keys. I don't know what his military schedule looks like."

Frowning, Alexa said, "I know, I was worried about that. But he'd want Mom to be with us, even if he couldn't be there with us."

"I'm sure," Matt soothed, "that if Dad can make it, he will. He doesn't have general's stars for nothing."

Gage met Alexa's shining gaze, loving the change in her. More than anything, he wanted this coming three-month sabbatical to be a time of healing for her. And if he had anything to do with it, he would give her all the love he had. Love, after all, was the greatest, most profound, natural medicine on earth.

THE BEGINNING...

Don't miss *Trapped*

Only from Lindsay McKenna and
Blue Turtle Publishing.

Available wherever you buy eBooks. Paperbacks
are available through CreateSpace/amazon.com,
and audiobooks through Tantor Media!

Read the sneak peek of *Trapped*!

Excerpt from

Trapped
by Lindsay McKenna

"GET THAT BITCH!" screamed Emilio Azarola, waving his Glock 18 in her direction.

Aliyana Montero spun around on her combat boots, grinning like the jaguar she was. Gripping the M4 in her gloved hand, she sped off into the woods of Mexico's Sierra Madre Mountains. That bastard Azarola, drug kingpin of the state of Sonora, had met his match today! She'd ambushed a four-vehicle convoy and taken out three of them with her RPG launcher. Millions of dollars of drugs just went up in those explosions.

Azarola knew her well, and this morning she wanted the sick bastard to know it was El Jaguar who ruled, not him. He'd given her this nickname two years ago, and she'd been a ghost in his life, making hit-and-run ops against his illegal business, costing him millions of dollars in lost and destroyed drugs. The CIA had hired her to do just that: work with the government of

Mexico to take the notorious Azarola down and capture him.

Now, she was close. *So close.* Wind tore past her as she dug the toes of her boots into the damp, October mountain soil. Above her, snow was already visible at the very top of this huge range. The soft soil beneath her boots and the pine needles sinking deep into the rich loam slowed her down as she raced through the woods to escape. Weaving in and out between the thickly forested trees, her hearing keyed to the sounds behind her, she heard more screams, curses, and shouts.

She'd created two huge explosions on the dirt road where she'd nailed the trucks filled with illegal drugs. The fire had reached the gas tanks, and the memory of that image made Ali smile. She was still breathing easily at eight-thousand feet because she was acclimated and familiar with the mountainous region. She'd lived here for two years, playing hide-and-seek with Azarola and his murderous soldiers. It gave her great pride to know she was making the drug lord hemorrhage money when he lost his cocaine packets, heroine, and huge bales of marijuana carried by those trucks. He had sent them off toward the US-Mexico border where they would have met other, smaller shipments, waiting on the other side.

The drivers would have divided up the drugs on the US side and then taken off in six different directions in the desert, each heading for big cities in the Southwest and California. There, the drugs would be sold to local dealers.

Not today, she grinned savagely, satisfaction thrumming through her as she raced across the landscape.

As she ran, her legs pumping, the forest-colored military cammos she wore helped her blend into the autumn landscape. It was cool at the higher reaches of the mountains, but her heart was elsewhere.

Cara, her twenty-six-year-old sister, had been kidnapped by Azarola's roving sex traffickers off the streets of Tucson, Arizona, a week ago. Ali had disobeyed direct CIA orders from her handler at Langley, and gone straight to Azarola's fortress high in the Sierra Madres. As a sniper, she had what was referred to as a 'hide.' It was where they hid from the enemy but could continue their recon activities. From her tree hide, she'd spotted her imprisoned sister with three other female, German tourists, all crowded into a small, outdoor cell. There were large tarps placed on top and draped down three sides of the cell where they'd been put. From a satellite, they couldn't be seen. But Ali had seen them with her binoculars as she sat hiding in a huge pine tree about twenty feet from Azarola's fortress. No one knew she was there because she was a sniper by training.

Sitting up in the tree, she'd spotted a soldier bring out a tray of food to the tarp enclosed prison. It was then she'd spotted Cara and the others. Ali had silently cried, her back against the huge pine tree, wanting so badly to go rescue her.

But she couldn't because her odds were terrible—one trained military woman against forty drug soldiers. She'd be killed if she tried to rescue them without a plan and a back-up team. Luckily, she worked with a company of Mexican Marines from an outpost in a nearby village. These men were the best of the best in that country's military. They'd teamed up with her often in the two years she'd been in the region. There were times they'd worked together to set traps for Azarola's men and trucks, nabbing the drivers and drugs. But they'd never won the grand prize: Azarola himself.

Maybe today.

Ali whipped in and around the trees, the wind now tearing past her. She could hear the drug soldiers huffing up the slope, far behind her. None of them was acclimated to this altitude like she was. Being able to outrun them was her ace in the hole, and now she was leading them into a trap where she hoped Azarola would finally be apprehended. Then, she could concentrate on getting her sister and her fellow captives released.

She knew that at some point, they would be driven to a container ship anchored at Puerto

Nuevo on the Pacific coast of the Baja Peninsula. From there, the ship would be bound for Asia, where the women would be sold as sex slaves.

The Books of Delos

Title: ***Last Chance*** (Prologue)
Publish Date: July 15, 2015
Learn more at:
delos.lindsaymckenna.com/last-chance

Title: ***Nowhere to Hide***
Publish Date: October 13, 2015
Learn more at:
delos.lindsaymckenna.com/nowhere-to-hide

Title: ***Tangled Pursuit***
Publish Date: November 11, 2015
Learn more at:
delos.lindsaymckenna.com/tangled-pursuit

Title: ***Forged in Fire***
Publish Date: December 3, 2015
Learn more at:
delos.lindsaymckenna.com/forged-in-fire

Title: *Broken Dreams*
Publish Date: January 2, 2016
Learn more at:
delos.lindsaymckenna.com/broken-dreams

Title: *Blind Sided*
Publish Date: June 5, 2016
Learn more at:
delos.lindsaymckenna.com/blind-sided

Title: *Secret Dream*
Publish Date: July 25, 2016
Learn more at:
delos.lindsaymckenna.com/secret-dream

Title: *Hold On*
Publish Date: August 3, 2016
Learn more at:
delos.lindsaymckenna.com/hold-on

Title: *Hold Me*
Publish Date: August 11, 2016
Learn more at
delos.lindsaymckenna.com/hold-me

Title: *Unbound Pursuit*
Publish Date: September 29, 2016
Learn more at:
delos.lindsaymckenna.com/unbound-pursuit

Title: *Secrets*
Publish Date: November 21, 2016
Learn more at:
delos.lindsaymckenna.com/secrets

Title: *Snowflake's Gift*
Publish Date: February 4, 2017
Learn more at:
delos.lindsaymckenna.com/snowflakes-gift

Title: ***Never Enough***
Publish Date: March 1, 2017
Learn more at:
delos.lindsaymckenna.com/never-enough

Everything Delos!

Newsletter

Please visit my newsletter website at newsletter.
lindsaymckenna.com. The newsletter will have
exclusive information about my books, publishing schedule, giveaways, exclusive cover peeks,
and more.

Delos Series Website

Be sure to drop by my website dedicated to the
Delos Series at delos.lindsaymckenna.com. There
will be new articles on characters, my publishing
schedule, and information about each book
written by Lindsay.

Made in the USA
Middletown, DE
14 December 2023

45628539R00116